PENGUIN BOOKS

© Philip O'Brien

Hamish Clayton was born in Hawke's Bay in
1977 and educated at Hastings Boys' High School.
He holds degrees in Art History and English
Literature from Victoria University of Wellington,
where he is currently working on a PhD in English
Literature. *Wulf* is his first novel.

WULF

Hamish Clayton

PENGUIN BOOKS

PENGUIN BOOKS
Published by the Penguin Group
Penguin Group (NZ), 67 Apollo Drive, Rosedale,
North Shore 0632, New Zealand (a division of Pearson New Zealand Ltd)
Penguin Group (USA) Inc., 375 Hudson Street,
New York, New York 10014, USA
Penguin Group (Canada), 90 Eglinton Avenue East, Suite 700, Toronto,
Ontario, M4P 2Y3, Canada (a division of Pearson Penguin Canada Inc.)
Penguin Books Ltd, 80 Strand, London, WC2R 0RL, England
Penguin Ireland, 25 St Stephen's Green,
Dublin 2, Ireland (a division of Penguin Books Ltd)
Penguin Group (Australia), 250 Camberwell Road, Camberwell,
Victoria 3124, Australia (a division of Pearson Australia Group Pty Ltd)
Penguin Books India Pvt Ltd, 11, Community Centre,
Panchsheel Park, New Delhi – 110 017, India
Penguin Books (South Africa) (Pty) Ltd, 24 Sturdee Avenue,
Rosebank, Johannesburg 2196, South Africa

Penguin Books Ltd, Registered Offices: 80 Strand, London, WC2R 0RL, England

First published by Penguin Group (NZ), 2011
1 3 5 7 9 10 8 6 4 2

Copyright © Hamish Clayton, 2011

The right of Hamish Clayton to be identified as the author of this work in terms of
section 96 of the Copyright Act 1994 is hereby asserted.

Hamer, Richard. *A Choice of Anglo-Saxon Verse: selected, with an introduction and a
parallel translation.* © 1970. Extract reprinted with permission of Faber and Faber Ltd.

Adams, John F. 'Wulf and Eadwacer: An Interpretation'. Modern Language
Notes 73:1 (1958), © 1958, The Johns Hopkins University Press. Reprinted with
permission of The Johns Hopkins University Press.

Cover design: Keely O'Shannessy
Cover illustrations: watercolours by Charles Heaphy, Alexander Turnbull Library:
sailing ship, 1850 (C-025-012); kākāriki, 1839 (C-025-007)

Designed by Anna Egan-Reid
Typeset by Pindar NZ
Printed in Australia by McPherson's Printing Group

All rights reserved. Without limiting the rights under copyright reserved above, no
part of this publication may be reproduced, stored in or introduced into a retrieval
system, or transmitted, in any form or by any means (electronic, mechanical,
photocopying, recording or otherwise), without the prior written permission of both
the copyright owner and the above publisher of this book.

ISBN 9780143206491

A catalogue record for this book is available
from the National Library of New Zealand.

www.penguin.co.nz

The assistance of Creative New Zealand towards the production of this book
is gratefully acknowledged by the Publisher.

In loving memory of Chris and Mark Clayton

To Kirsten, with thanks

For Rosie

Contents

Sometime in the tenth century, or perhaps earlier, a poet somewhere in Britain wrote a poem which has come to be known as both 'Wulf' and 'Wulf and Eadwacer'. Famously cryptic, its obscure narrative describes a female speaker's yearning for a man called Wulf, though her relationship to him is deeply ambiguous. While it has been suggested that Wulf and Eadwacer could form, with the speaker, the respective points of an adulterous triangle, other interpretations insist that Wulf and Eadwacer are one and the same, and still others that the speaker's distress is in fact a mother's lament for a son slain in battle, or a dead child. A final, agreed interpretation seems unlikely, for, as well as privileging dense allusion and raw emotion over strict narrative coherence, the poem resists smooth translation: the Old English word for 'gift' can also mean 'play' or 'battle'; the word for 'destroy' can be used to mean 'receive'; and the word for 'feed' or 'serve' can also mean 'kill'. Further, the wolf of the last stanza need not necessarily refer to the character Wulf, while the name Eadwacer, possibly meaning 'cradle-watcher', 'home-watcher', or 'guardian of valuables', might be another name for Wulf himself. Appropriately, the final line's word for 'song' has also, on occasion, been interpreted to mean 'riddle'. Regardless of how the poem is read, there can be no denying either its enduring mystery or its tone of lasting, bitterest despair.

Almost a thousand years after 'Wulf and Eadwacer' was written in Britain, the warrior chief Te Rauparaha of the tribe Ngāti Toa rose to dominate the tribal structure of the pre-colonial Māori in New Zealand.

It is as though my people have been given
A present. They will wish to capture him
If he comes with a troop. We are apart.
Wulf is on one isle, I am on another.
Fast is that island set among the fen.
Murderous are the people who inhabit
That island. They will wish to capture him
If he comes with a troop. We are apart.
Grieved have I for my Wulf with distant longings.
Then it was rainy weather, and I sad,
When the bold warrior laid his arms about me.
I took delight in that and also pain.
O Wulf, my Wulf, my longing for your coming
Has made me ill, the rareness of your visits,
My grieving spirit, not the lack of food.
Eadwacer, do you hear me? For a wolf
Shall carry to the woods our wretched whelp.
Men very easily may put asunder
That which was never joined, our song together.

Translated by Richard Hamer

I.

Entry

I never saw in all my wide-wanderings a country so fresh, so harsh, so beauteous-green. I never set foot in any country so bitter-cold in the middle months. July and August, such cold-bitten jewels. So they felt to us. Our northern skins.

That country lay in far and unstable waters. History lay in wait for that far and unstable country.

Every word spoken, sent like a raft of smoke onto the air of that strange country, smelled like the blood riding the breath of their great chief, fearful to us, the Southern Napoleon. Amongst ourselves we'd taken to calling him the Great Wolf, for the men imagined him falling upon us when our backs were turned, creating a cloak of darkness, shadowy like an animal's hide, out of which he would attack, the spear in his hand like a bone, the spirit inside him burning. We knew he was coming. At the fall of the

evening we knew he was coming. We could feel his breath
on the frozen air.

He was an entertainment and a terror we told beside
fires, between sheets of rum, at the passing of tobacco in
the evenings. Our fear held us and told us he was coming.
Everything we didn't know about that country held us and
told us he was coming.

Out there in the night we could hear the sounds of
    birds
Their sounds were strange sounds
Those nights were strange nights

Near the start of 1830, towards the end of February, we
left London in the merchant brig *Elizabeth*. Laden with the
daydreams of trade, the lands of myth ahead of us, we
rode trade-winds and the whale-road. We set our sails for
the South Seas, for the ends of the earth, for those colonies
that were becoming New southern countries that weren't
countries yet: New Holland and New South Wales. New
Zealand, whose islands would later be named New Ulster,
New Munster and New Leinster. Colonies yet to be that
looked back over the shoulder of the earth to see Home.

We sailed south, the boat a great armchair rocking on
the spot though we knew we were falling slowly around
the surface of the earth. In only a few months we had
sailed from our northern winter through the savage heat
at the belt of the globe to another winter at the bottom

of the world. We felt the enormous weight of the planet, a ball spinning beneath the tread of our brig, the seasons capsizing around us.

We arrived in Sydney in the rain in the night. We looked at Gunn's maps of the Australian country, a whole continent the shape of a bison. On those maps Sydney was a paper-weight holding that great island down in the ocean. The steady, ancient earth. But our captain pointed to those other islands, far smaller and wilder, further south and east, that moved like driftwood on the tide of the Pacific. Those islands, restless with earthquakes we'd heard, were being called New Zealand. Those islands pulled like an angry fish on a line, like a wild dog on a leash. They were the last place on earth and our captain said, we are going over there to trade, men. Or he said we are going over there to trade men.

In August we left Sydney. We crossed the ditch of ocean that lay between Australia and New Zealand called the Tasman Sea. Though it was winter there, that was a mild sea till we were more than halfway across it. Then the season started snapping its salty teeth and through the cold rainy air we came upon the islands of New Zealand: New Ulster in the North, New Munster in the South, the final, broken shelf of the planet.

To the South its sides
rose steeply from the sea,
as steep as the green sides of a ship
whose timber sides were turned green
by the sea.

To the North it lay
as flat as an animal that lay
in the water, watching us watching it
as we approached,
entering its water.

The country lay like a gift from the open sky before us.

When we landed we realised they'd seen us before, others
like us, earlier traders, whalers. They knew us from the
thin colour of our skins. Our strange boots. Our muddy
eyes and beards. We had not landed among war-like
ones, though they knew the craft of war. They welcomed
us. From earlier traders, whalers, they knew about our
customs in ways that impressed us. We moved among
them, keeping our distance, mindful. They knew our
habits: our need to get drunk in the evenings, our love
of songs and the fire. Our wish to trade. Our muskets for
their flax, our rum for their flax, our tobacco for their flax.
Our flints wrapped in blankets. Our sea-calloused men's
hands for the smooth round hips of their women and
girls. Their warm brown shades. Our white flesh, at sea for
months, tasted of salt to them. We gave them meat and
took handfuls of arse and breast. They were game. Our
desire for trade, so rampant, our minds and bodies thick
with it – our desire for trade always turned to the business
of fucking.

We were wary of them, but more wary of putting

down roots, of planting ourselves there. Going native was the concern.

There was a madness that grew from that earth, those strange trees that grew in dark wet gullies: black and green, the sun-shattered leaves that stayed green on the trees through the cold of winter. The madness of that winter light: in the late afternoon it lay low and orange, pouring shadows into gullies like basins, empty and overflowing, everything made into black wet shadows. And deep in those gullies, opening like arms and legs as black and green and wet as the great trees that grew from deep inside them, and whose roots grew from a stomach of stars inside the earth, everything was as black as the stomach of a tree. The black green trees. The black trees green. We were wary of everything there.

The madness that grew from inside that land grew quickest when the shadows grew long, like snakes crawling from the corners of the earth, though we knew there were no snakes crawling through those islands. If there was a madness growing from out of that earth, then it was a madness that grew from our own imaginations, for we'd stowed these away with us during the long months at sea, brought them ashore like handfuls of seed or dirt and then scattered them like accidental traces of ourselves in the soil of these new islands.

One evening I felt that madness come upon me, its cool green fingers becoming my fingers, its shaded eyes becoming my eyes.

I had been walking through gullies through the afternoon, through sheer green gullies, through wild green rooms. Those forests were dense and ancient forests. They could barely be moved through except by following their rivers or occasional paths already made. For the land there steers the man walking through it, and when he finds a path to follow then the terrain itself seems to have been already sliced by another mind. Yet it is always the land that steers him.

After many hours, when I had walked through many strange valleys, the light became suddenly cool and thin like water, and I realised that the sun had fallen away beyond the western edge of the world. In the quickly fading light I hurried to find my way back through that unsettling country. That was a fearsome-terrible hour for me, for as the light was drained from the forest the green world I'd been within suddenly became dark and colourless, and I felt submerged, underwater. And though I could look up and see, through the trees, a sky which was – even then, beautiful, coloured – not yet night, everything beneath my feet and before my body was confusing, made of ink. The land regarded me through its dark guard of trees, sinister eyes invisible within their branches, and everything moved around me as I moved through that landscape, my breath held like a silent paddle.

I came to a sloping path plunging into the heart of a very deep cleft in the side of the earth which, I was sure, I had neither walked through nor seen that afternoon. But it was heading in what I took to be my direction – north-east – as well as uphill, towards what remained of the day, out of those hideous gullies, and I began to breathe again as I climbed its gentle slope. And as I walked I looked to the sky above me, to be cheered again by the beauty of the pure evening shade and the reminder of the day within it. When I looked back down to look along the path before me, I froze and every drop of blood inside me turned to ice.

Thirty feet off, to the side of the path, crouched the black shape of a large Wolf, facing me, watching me, and even in that second which had split and stopped me straight and dead in my tracks I cursed myself a bloody fool – for now the animal had surely seen me, guessed that I had spotted it having seen my sudden stop, and would be upon my throat in a moment.

And inside that broken second I thought how, it was supposed, there were no wolves on those islands. So we'd been told. But I was once a hunter in the north of the world, on islands far away from these, and I know the shape of a Wolf in the twilight as it sits on the edge of its dark country. I know the shape of a Wolf that is watching and waiting and I know the shape of its leap, made in the air when the line of protection is crossed. This is a line it wears against itself, between itself and the world like the outline of its own body. For the Wolf is an animal of line, and is made of lines: a stripe in the fur, curves of tooth and claw, triangles of ear, shelves of paw. A whisker. These keep the Wolf from becoming something else in the world, and yet they are only a conspiracy of lines. In the dark places of strange lands outlines make a shape we can name, a beginning and an ending we recognise even within shadows at the far end of the earth.

All these things I thought in the broken chamber of a single second. And even as I thought them I knew they were madness. No Wolf I had encountered had ever leaped at me, save one which had been rabid, mad. The creature that crouched before me was too still, too composed, for such animal insanity to be buried within its folds of flesh and fur. I found my fear cooling like an ember where previously there had been flame and crept carefully forward. And though the Wolf still did not move, it changed before my eyes, so as I stepped gradually closer it became clearer to me and miraculously I saw two things held within the same shape: a Wolf – its pointed ears, its sloping back – and a broken, blackened tree-stump. A tree-stump! Erupting from out of the earth at an angle like a twisted tooth. As soon as I saw that stump for what it was, relief came like a flood within me. I laughed out loud but the sound, as flat and empty as coins dropped into a tin bucket, quickly died in the cold air. I went to the stump and stood over it and saw how hollow it was, the faint green colour about its lichen flanks. The Wolf had vanished. I patted its head behind its two wooden ears and laughed again, and again the gully killed my laughter.

I hurried on up the path until I broke the surface of the forest and I felt then as though I was coming up for air. It was lighter there, out of the trees on the ridge overlooking the forest-thick hide of the earth. Behind me the sunset an orange scar. A bright star hung in the east. I followed it home. A short walk to our camp.

The next day I woke early. Edward Walker, the night-watch, was sitting beside the fire in the cool morning, quietly smoking his pipe. I said good morning and asked him if he'd ever seen a New Zealand wolf. No such animal he spat and I said I could show him one. So we left our camp unguarded and I led him away till we stood on a familiar ridge of land. We found the same path I'd used the evening before to climb from the same cleft of hillside into which we descended, but there was no broken stump of tree anywhere along the way. For an hour or more we walked, but I could find no Wolf. Walker must have thought me mad, my talk of wolves and eyeing of tree-stumps.

We turned to walk back and the rain came. Though we could hear the wind high above the ridges all around us we were well sheltered as we went. While we walked I told Walker of what I had seen the previous night on those very paths, the tree-stump in the shape of a Wolf. He listened in silence. By the time we returned the others had been awake for a couple of hours. They asked us where we'd been. 'I thought I saw Wolves,' Walker said flatly, and the men laughed and the captain said, 'Night-watch for ten nights, Walker.' Walker spat and said he would not be the watch for the next ten nights – and he was right – but from then on he was always called the Watcher.

I walked alone through that gully again, searching without finding the tree-stump broken into the shape of a Wolf. One evening, the last we were camped in that corner of the country, I went walking, sure that I would find the treasured glimpse I sought if I walked during the correct hour. If I walked when the hour was late enough and not too late. If I walked when the sun was gone but the sky still remembered it. If I walked when the light was almost drained from the sky and the shadows were walking the valleys themselves. Still I saw no Wolf, no stump of tree to bend the human eye.

But again I found myself submerged in the inky dusk and climbing towards the surface of light above the forest, the earth climbing sheer on either side of the path as if the unforgiving sides of a great ship. And a faint whisper of my terror came on me again when suddenly I saw, shining in the black earth all around me, dozens of stars, the midnight sky contained beneath the roots of strange trees. Their trunks rose from the utter darkness of the earth before my eyes and parted to become a black net of branches holding the twilight sky above me. I stopped there and took in this vision of the planet, double-skied. Beneath the trees, the sky. Above the trees, the sky. And though I knew the stars inside the earth to be glowing worms or insects I felt I was a stranger to the order of things. So again I left that gully as quickly as I could. I climbed out of those trees and was relieved to make our camp.

That night while we drank I sat staring into the fire and the captain said we were sailing for Entry Island to trade for flax. The men looked at Gunn's maps. We saw Entry, a chipped tooth off the bottom of the Northern Island. We knew who was there on that island.

While the men told stories I stared into the fire. If I was the first to tell the story of a Wolf in those forests then I was the first among us to bring wolves to that country. Later, after we'd renamed their great warrior chief in those animals' honour, our captain – a fool – would claim to have brought a Wolf aboard, stowed in the hold and carried between islands. (Even later, at the court in Sydney, he would change his story. No matter.) In the time we were there we made that country from stories of creatures which had never set foot upon it, had never stalked its black valleys. Had never preyed on its lambs or children. Had never dampened their paws in its Roman rivers. We were on our islands; wolves were on another. We were new islands, anchors at the bottom of the world; wolves were old islands, hands reaching down to us, to this country we were making with the memory of animals which had never been there. I stared until I felt as though I was made of fire.

This is what held me: a tree like a bucket, balanced
      on the sky and holding the sky
And this is what led me: the shape of a tree-stump,
      mistaken for and making a Wolf
And this is what sheltered me: the side of a hill as dry
      as a brother's side, a cow's flank in a land without
      cattle, as dry as the inside of a wooden ship
And all of this is what drove me.

I dreamed of an island covered in ice. The white sea. There was an earthquake and the sea was made into writhing shelves, an enormous basin opening in the ocean, the back of a giant sea-monster rolling over before us – the island behind, rock-broken and snow-covered, its frozen teeth in the sky, regarding us with its anger. Later, when we drew near to Entry Island, that the natives call Kopitee, I saw it and said, 'That is the island I dreamed of.' The others said, 'But it is low and green. The island you dreamed of was made of ice.' And I said, 'That is the island I dreamed of.'

That was later, but for now we sailed. For now we had days of blue sun.

II.

The Source of the Nile

'I've had most my life on the sea but this I've always
known: it will be a foreign river that takes me in the end.'

This from Cowell, the ship's trading master, who could
speak with the New Zealanders in their native tongue. He
had a recurring river fantasy, a terror that held him.

Cowell is on the bank of a deep green river. He is walking
over stones, beside the flat and slow-moving surface of
the water which carries upon itself, unbroken, the vast
clear reflections of the trees and sky behind. The river is
a tapestry, a sheet of painted green glass, moving. Leaves
have fallen onto its skin and become rafts, gliding on the
cool, slow body of water. Beside such a river he feels as
though he is walking a dog on a lead.

After a time the river narrows, forcing the current
to quicken, the dog of water bounding ahead of him
splashing on its leash. The stony banks on either side
become sheer banks of dense trees and rock. There is

no place left to walk if he wishes to continue along its course, and so laughing he enters the water, fully clothed and wearing the river around his knees, wading with the current. He becomes both the river and the dog swimming within it. He becomes both water and paddle. As the water-road deepens, the flow quickens and his feet slip on the slimy floor of rocks so he flies and is swept down the river. He is churning water, tossed and surging and out of control and his thoughts become a sudden terror: he visualises invisible blades and axes when his feet knock the roots of trees and sunken logs that wait, cold and silent, beneath the torrent. He imagines this underwater world into existence: hard and unmoving in the rampant water below, a buried grave of ancient war, the blades waiting to smash his dangling limbs, to shatter the bone and quarter his body, to slice the flesh of his feet into bloody paws.

He cannot escape the river.

We were slowly making our way south, down the side of the island like a hand down a lover's body, occasionally venturing inland, ashore. Cowell went and came away from the island with stories. His head spilling like a bucket.

We heard stories of New Zealand gold. But this gold was not the gold we knew: it was not dragon-hoard or serpent's lair, vaulted inside a rocky earth warmed by its yellow gleam. It grew in rivers and greeted the eye a deep green as if made from the swirl of the mountain waters in which it was forged. The natives wore it in their hair and about their necks and they fashioned it into bladed weapons. Green-stone, a Jewel of War, we called it.

The gold that we knew, the old-gold, had no value in that country. And yet we knew it was there – Cowell had seen the native children playing their children's games in the dirt with golden nuggets. We told him to obtain a few and he did. When he brought them to us we bit into them and broke our teeth and we saw that they were real. And so we dreamed of the gold running through the veins of the islands, untouched, undiscovered, and waiting for us. We were sure there would be rushes for gold later, when we knew the islands better, when we'd tamed their wild green hillsides, their treacherous tree-clad mountains. But the New Zealanders already knew that our white hearts and minds were made of that heavy yellow metal. They boasted to Cowell that they threw large rocks of it back into the rivers from which the bullion came, for it was worthless to them. Cowell asked them which rivers.

When they asked him to explain the value of gold he gave them the oldest stories he knew, strange poems from the islands of northern seas about a warrior-king Cowell called the Bee-Wolf. Through such obscure trinkets he could explain the burial of gold inside the earth to the natives in ways that appealed to them, for he understood how they saw the earth as a store of all that was valuable in the world.

'There was an old man among the New Zealanders whose hair had turned white and whose teeth had turned brown, but whose black eyes sparkled as brightly as polished stones. He listened intently all through my stories, nodding and smiling and whistling at the monsters

27

I'd made, at the feats of their slaying. He knew about dragons, understanding they must be fought and killed. He understood the sadness of gold, sighing when I told him of mead-halls. When my stories ended he rose to his feet and limped across to me. With one bony hand he gripped my shoulder like a pincer and with the other he pointed to the small trees growing nearby. In the local tongue these trees are called kaw-fy: "yellow". I had noticed them earlier, for their yellow-flowered limbs, empty of leaves, are unusual in a country where each tree seems ever-green and fully-leaved. The old man held me there and smiled and asked me, "What does the white-skinned goblin suppose lies buried beneath the yellow tree?" I did not understand his question but he was patient with me. He clicked his tongue and sucked his lips and looked at me intently, and asked in his old voice, cracked as an old oak table, "Do these trees grow from soil where gold lies hidden in the earth? Is that why this tree bears yellow flowers?" I did not know how to answer him. I stood there dumbly and he said he had seen me eyeing the little yellow tree with a curious regard, me with my strange fair skin and my hardened yellow heart. I stayed quiet and he went on, his bright, intelligent eyes staring through me as he spoke. "What of all these other trees?" he asked me, waving his free hand around us. "Do you see how green they are? Do you see that it is our green-stone that lies buried in the earth? That is forged in the rivers?" And then the smile on the old man's face faded and his grip on my shoulder tightened. "Do not bring your gold to this land," he said. "Do not bury your gold here in this country of green trees and dark mountain waters, for when you hide your treasure in this soil, then we will fight wars for the land. We will open your white heads and your hot blood will be poured into the earth and the leaves of the trees that grow from the crying ground will turn red, watered by your blood." And then he leaned so close to me that I could feel his breath fill my mouth and he said to me, "I have dreamed that one day you will bring your trees to this land. You will plant them over your buried gold and your fallen dead. Your trees will turn this green country into seasons of yellow and red." He continued to hold me by the shoulder, looking into my eyes to see that I had understood.'

We heard these stories and sat quietly. We looked about us in the dark.

Cowell swore he had not told the old man of the European trees whose colours, turning with the seasons, we missed amongst ourselves. 'Not a word of it,' he said. 'Not so much as an English acorn. Not a single autumn-coloured leaf.' We half believed him. He said he believed the old man to be a prophet. We did not believe him.

'A raving cannibal,' muttered Clementson. 'A savage driven mad by the taste of too much human meat.' Cowell pretended not to hear, Clementson being the chief mate on board.

We enjoyed Cowell's stories. His tendency to pull them suddenly from hidden pockets like card tricks beside the fire.

'The old man has a fascination for the maps. He thought they were illustrations of the ancestors we had brought with us over the sea. I explained that the maps were drawings of the land, not people, and he cackled and replied: There is no difference between the land and the people.

'This evening I perused my book of maps and was struck by the outline of Africa. Does it not, on the map, rather resemble the outline of a human skull? Or a mummified head, viewed in profile? Doesn't the eastern coast descend like a nose into contours of lips? Isn't that the chin just there at the Cape? The full and heavy pouch of brain in the north-west corner? Those men now wandering and hunting the source of the Nile, dreaming of a lake large beyond imagining, should read their unfinished maps of the Dark Continent as if a human head. For where better to couch the socket of all life on that vast dry shelf than where we would expect to find the human eye on such a map? Here is the eye, the source of the Nile.'

And Cowell sketched quickly before us a shape we recognised to be a map of Africa, the Nile like a lock of wet hair running slick against its forehead or a split in the skull. Near its eastern coast, inland from the bridge of the nose, he drew in a triangle of lake, which appeared on no other map at that time, small enough to make an eye and large enough for the whole continent to stare out forever across the Indian Ocean. A river marked where his map supposed the Nile to continue to flow into the far south of Africa, a tear making the contoured cheek, gathering in the glen of lip.

'I made a gift of maps for the old man. I had told him the world was round, like an orange. He looked at the maps that lay flat, spread out on the ground, and laughed at me like a parent laughs at a misguided child. "The world is round like a plate," he assured me. But he took the maps from me. The next day when I visited him I was ushered into his hut with great excitement. The hut was small and smoky and there was barely room for two men. As my eyes became used to the darkness, I saw that he'd plastered our maps to the walls of his hovel. Portraits of nations and seas slowly emerged, approaching me from out of the dark. He walked slowly about the room with one hand against its continuous side, a muddy wall becoming another wall, the next, the next, and back to the first. From Europe his brown palm moved across the Atlantic to America; across the Pacific to Asia. His hand passed over Asia until it felt Europe again. So he'd realised how the world can seem flat but continuously return to itself. And yet he'd made a model of the world that worked in reverse, a globe looking inward. Later I took one of our globes from the ship and gifted this to him as well. He put that in the middle of the floor of his hut. So now the real globe sits inside the model of the world he'd made, a brain inside a skull, a nut within a shell. I am pleased to have given him such a gift, double-sided, whose horizons endlessly translate, one into the other.'

Cowell occasionally taught us snatches of the local tongue. We got tangled in its net of strange sounds. Teach me something useful, said Clementson. Teach me to say, 'You are a very beautiful woman.' So Cowell sounded out a small phrase slowly. And again, more slowly. The words, every drop, were passed between their mouths, from Cowell into Clementson. Over the next few days Clementson walked about the boat with the mantra of unfamiliar syllables, unaware of the particular words he was reciting but carrying the whole phrase like a string of strange pearls. Clementson like a child held in the net of his concentration.

On other days we heard him complaining about the maps and the globe that strangely, suddenly, had gone missing from his cabin.

Our position.

We sailed our sheets between the savages, down the western coast of the Northern Island – not yet called New Ulster – and we saw that this island was an island of war, native blood running openly from its throat. We had muskets so we thought we were safe enough, though it was not the protection of firearms that fixed our safety. It was because the New Zealand savages coveted the musket that we sailed as if beyond a veil separating the worlds of ghosts and men. We were sacred to them. Our muskets were not fires made of steel sweeping clear our trade-road before us, but the diamonds of war, desired and beautiful. We were not feared. We were usable, useful to them. They wished to trade and they traded honourably. They sought the devils we brought as protection from their own gods of plunder.

I wondered which gods they prayed to. They'd arrived here in this country before God had even thought of it. This was a country overlooked by God.

<hr />

One evening when we were moored near the shore I entered Cowell's cabin. He was not there, though it took a moment to see the room was empty. His cabin was always untidy. He had taken to collecting, among other curios, dead native birds; a brace lay on the small table beside his bunk. I saw their dark glossy feathers, their inky black shining blue and green in the shifting light of the late afternoon. Late orange sunlight slanted into the room and fell in a wedge upon the table where the birds lay as though waiting in a butcher's shambles. A club of white feathers like a pair of berries sprouted from each of the birds' throats. Their delicate claws curled in death. My attention lay there for a few moments, for the plumage of these birds contained the colours and lights of the forests from which they came. After a short time, wary of being found alone in another's cabin, I turned to go. But as I moved I glimpsed a lock of black hair, a long trail spilling over the side of the bunk from beneath the bunched sheets. I thought Cowell must have brought a native girl aboard, or a young boy, and I froze while I stared at that hair, trying to tell whether it belonged to a body that lay sleeping or awake. After a few moments I could see no movement at all, and so I crept forward, curious and sure that the body lay in the very deepest of sleeps. When I lifted the sheet I beheld the native tattooed head of a grown man, severed, its eyes and mouth sewn shut. The hair had begun to loosen from the top-knot into which it had been carefully arranged, tied there with albatross feathers. I regarded it for a few moments before I put the sheet back over the head resting at the foot of the bunk, the bunk where Cowell slept, and I left the cabin. Afterwards I tried not to remember that hideous nest.

But the sight of that head had removed something from within me. In the days following I felt a space, a cavity in my chest, filling with a pool of new knowledge and whatever lack had emerged inside me, I felt too a desire to replace it with a bone of resistance. I needed to measure the will within me and I took to walking further inland when I walked on shore alone. I desired the heart of the country. I needed to move through the landscape of my curiosity. I sought the biblical rivers of that country, so that I might cross them or else choose not to cross them. The country's secrets lay behind the hands of its rivers.

Secrets of leaves.

I walked and I came upon a river too wide to cross. It was green and slow-moving and I was reminded of the foreign river of Cowell's imagining. I wished to inhabit Cowell's body and all the stories contained within him. I wished to trade my knowledge for his, and I realised I had found the source of the river before me, and perhaps all rivers, to be contained within my desire for such places, hidden from view, as old as anything on the globe, but ancient and new. This river began flowing from the eye that first beheld it, from a tear made against the earth.

I undressed and bathed there. My sea-salty skin washed in the fresh water. I became a white rock firm in the midst of flowing water and wondered whether I was the first white man to bathe there. I had an urge to spend myself inside a woman though there was no woman in mind. The moment came and passed and I left the river when I was emptier of such hunger, my body cooler, my hands cleaned by the water, my white desire washed away downstream, dispersed into those green waters. I stood on the bank naked, drying, the New Zealand sun a paw over my whole body for the first time.

I left the river and wandered back the way I came.

III.

The Whale-Road

John Vittoria Cowell. He had a mind as warm and nimble as a pair of hands in fingerless mittens. His quiet curiosity bent towards everything around him. His gaze was the steadiest gaze of any man on ship.

One morning, when the clouds were thick but scattered and torn open, standing still though the brig rolled and pitched, a wooden cradle beneath our feet, Cowell, his eyes never leaving a lighter patch in the grey distance of the sea, said quietly, 'Whales out there, several pairs.' We looked to where the sunlight rested on the water, a few bands of shining steel lying thin and flat far off on the silver-duned sea. Half a minute or so later fountains of whale's breath appeared, miles away. Two spouts of white spray then more, the water-dust rising and becoming a forest. Over a dozen I counted.

Cowell was not quiet by nature but he carried surprises like these black whales, drifting like barges on our horizons: surprises that surfaced and then mesmerised us into silence. Walker, the Watcher, said he imagined hidden doubloons smuggled about Cowell's body, among his oilskins, just as I'd often thought about the exotic treasure of his middle name.

Although he was the youngest on board, Cowell had been in New Zealand before. He was the first among us, the last among us.

I began to love him and all the possibilities of knowledge that hung from him. I started to notice his hands, admiring their swiftness with knots, the knuckles of fingers and thumbs coinciding with twists of rope. I watched him in his deftness from behind or beside him, noticing the twitch in the shell of bone just beneath the ear. The softness of skin just back from his jaw, a place he never had to shave.

He moved the rope around my relaxed hands, fastening them together suddenly so the cord bit into my flesh, a graze of teeth, the hands held tightly in those jaws, then jerking the bonds so they fell away slack, harmless to the floor, the violent mind within them removed. A snake-charmer in a land without snakes.

Did you see that time?

No. Again.

He tied my hands again.

He told me his father was a rope-maker.

Cowell knew too much for a young man. We did not know – no one on board knew, I am sure – the precision of his years. He was the youth among us, yet he used his way of speaking, his knowledge, to arm himself against youth. He barricaded himself from the taunts of the older men behind his calm confidence with the principles of languages, of trade. The knowledge of gold and song, the behaviour of ropes and whales. A comfort with rum which feigned the weathering of the years. He was too young for the cynicism of a man who foresaw his own death at the hands of a wild river. He was too young to have claimed a life lived mainly on the sea.

He had joined our crew late, shipping with us only from Sydney. Previously he'd sailed two trading voyages with the *Harlequin* to New Zealand, acting as the interpreter on board, coming under the command of the captains Scott and Monteith. They vouched loudly for him. 'As good as having a native,' they said. 'Born with a brown tongue in his head,' said Scott. 'Silver-tongued as well,' muttered Monteith. So Cowell joined us as supercargo. When he crossed the Tasman Sea with us he made his fifth crossing in seven months. It would be his last crossing.

Cowell explained the whale-road we followed down the side of the island, for he'd observed the favoured paths and the pace of its traffic. Whales arrived off the northern coasts in May, as the country thought about rolling over into its frozen winter blankets. The whales had already treaded the waters we now trod, had already swum south as we now sailed south, through waters west of the country. They had already passed between the mainland of the Northern Island and Entry Island. That slim fast wrist of water, that slipping highway. By June they had mostly passed between the Northern and Middle Islands, New Ulster in the north, New Munster in the south, swimming through Cook's Straits. That water was the waist of the country. Beyond it, the whale-road forked into separate legs and became cooler. Some whales moved far out to the eastern side of the southerly Middle Island while others traversed the western side, to calve in the far southern bays of New Zealand. Anywhere along these whale-roads, anywhere they passed close to coasts, calving whales might be found. Cowell had eaten with the frozen hard-bitten men who kept the first whaling stations along these sea-roads.

'Too many whales this far north for September,' muttered Richardson.

'An omen,' Cowell said.

'An omen of what?'

'Better not to ask. Better not to know.'

We were only heading as far south as Entry. We had no desire for whatever lay further ahead on the whale-road. We had no desire for omens.

I desired moments alone with Cowell. I stole these when I could. I pressed him for the stories he had learned which would explain the green rainforests of this other planet. The warrior-chiefs who took their names from the colour of their own breath in the cold steel mornings, the light falling on hillsides, or the tail-feathers of long-extinct birds. After months at sea I needed to draw fresh water from Cowell, from the deep well of stories within him. I wanted to lie in his rivers.

When I went ashore and walked alone through those tangled forests, following the splashing threads of rushing streams, stepping across the wide green beds of broken rocks at the bottom of deep gullies I was a man in search of Cowell's stories. That landscape was alive with the touch of a curious mind, though I could not tell whether it was his or mine. Perhaps I believed then that our minds were one and the same. Perhaps that was why I became the villain I did, entering his cabin when he was not there and searching his things. I found his journal and read from it, unsure and unable to guess if the fragments and stories I read there were stories he had plundered or invented. And if they were stories told to him by his friends among the natives I had no way of telling the accuracy of translation. And yet I was drawn to them, compelled by their utter strangeness, as I was drawn to the tattooed head, now housed in a wooden box carved in the curiously curving patterns favoured by the native artisans. This box was itself a thing of high and strange beauty, and though I knew nothing of such arts I reckoned the New Zealanders to rank among the most careful and consistent of craftsmen whose handiwork I had ever seen. Three times I entered the cabin to read from Cowell's journal and three times I drew the box from beneath the bunk where I knew the head was hidden. I held it in my hands and took its weight. I felt its treasure inside, the heavy rock of a human head, its soft thud against the dark native timber. Although Cowell had tied its lid fast with a fine flax rope, three times I undid this knot. Three times I lifted the wooden cover and beheld the carved flesh of the face inside. And three times, before I left, Cowell's knot I carefully retied.

New Zealand Work Song. (Heard sung by men at the sweet
potato patch, sometime early in 1829. Northern bays of the
Northern Island.):

    Deceive, deceive, deceive the man,
    Flatter, flatter, flatter the woman,
    Work and work until the work is done.
    Then you may sleep. Asleep in the place of sleep,
    Your body, spread out, makes dreams of how the earth
        was born.

New Zealanders' Jeering Song. (Sung by many tribes
throughout the Northern Island and inspired by a terrifying
chief of the central and western districts. Translated
Feb. 1830):

    Seek out the goodness of that plant; do not forget
        its name!
    Convolvulus growing in the sand near the sea; do not
        forget its name!
    He may be good to eat,
    He may be bad to eat,
    But do not forget he may cause blindness, do not forget
        his name!

I found these snatches of poems that Cowell had discovered
and plucked from this dark corner of the earth. I found
them pressed between the pages of his journal like exotic

moths, rare plants. They could have been the last poems to be found in the world. Wild and uncultivated they'd thrived in this green and black country for hundreds of years, growing like its wet forests from which trees were cut by teeth of savage stone, their dark hard woods carved into figures made to guard houses and canoes-of-war. And when Cowell came to them did he come to them as another craftsman or as a harvester, a wandering gatherer of wild crops? He had turned a spade over them and removed them from their home of damp black earth, he had wiped them clean like new potatoes. He'd handled them gently and laid them out on a clean white sheet. He'd broken their lines carefully. Yet I felt too the uncertain angles of translated words. I saw the shadows of fish moving swiftly beneath the surface of the water he'd written upon. Meaning shifted sideways, disappearing into the outline of space it was contained by, leaving an echo of itself in the cold air that seemed more real than it had ever really been.

Cowell's handwriting lay as strong and shapely as a fine rope, a thread, heavy and dark on the page.

My life was a storm made out of the wind and the rain of two women. I kept them on separate islands, my women. I made gifts out of them, from the bodies of them, and I gave gifts between them, so they were passed between, from one woman to the other though they did not know it. I kept this from them for they were jealous of one another being alike in beauty. Older men told me I was foolish to keep two such beautiful wives, for women were better when they knew the worth of their faces. I should have had one beautiful and another not so beautiful for then there should have been less jealousy. Instead I shared the days between them, on their separate islands; I spent the days paddling between my wives.

I slept beside my shining star and in the mornings woke next to her. One morning when I went from her she said to me: Take this gourd and fill it with the water from the stream which flows beside this village. Drink of the gourd when you are thirsty on your journey to yonder island. And before you leave that village, before you return to me, fill the gourd from the strange waters that flow there. Then I will know that you have water to drink when you are thirsty and as you paddle back to me.

So I filled the gourd with water and carried it with me on my journey as she had said, but I did not drink it. I saved that water and when I arrived on the island of my evening star, my other wife who lived there, I gave the gourd to her as a gift, saying to her: I have brought this water from my other island so that you may feed and nourish the sweet potatoes that grow beside your village. Because this water comes from me and is part of me, then it is as though the flesh of the potatoes will be my flesh, and when you consume them you will consume me.

And then my evening star said to me: Take young cuttings from the great trees which grow deep in the gullies between these hills and on their steep sides and when you return to your other island grow them there in that strange soil so my shade and light will be upon you, even on that other island. So I took these saplings and when I returned to my other island I gave the young trees to my other wife, my morning star, my morning love, saying that I came to her with a gift of trees.

44

In this way gifts passed between them through me. In this way I made gifts for the one from the other. My life was a storm made out of the wind and the rain of two women.

I smiled and wondered whose women these were. I wondered which native chief it was who'd owned them like two fine feather cloaks. I wanted to look on the face of such a chief. I wanted Cowell to take me into the dark heart of the country, to lead me into the landscape of trees contained in his journals, their inky shapes as black as pitch against a wounded sky, pale yellow in the evening. I wanted to look on lakes and harbours grey and blue and flat beneath the weight of frozen purple clouds, the wide shape of water wind-beaten in my imagining as though it had been hammered in a Viking smithy. I wanted the black thighs of hills rising out of those harbours around me.

There were times I thought I was going native. There were times I felt the animal pull of those lush green islands. When I walked through a quiet forest and came to a river and lay within it, unclothed and held in its cold caress of rushing water. When I lay there and worked and spent myself into the native river. When I wanted to be found, naked and hard and helpless, by women with skins as brown as exotic fruit. When I felt a country made of dark trees and shadows and when I felt the dark trees and shadows resisting the shape of the country which we thought we'd entered. When I slipped into Cowell's journals, when I edged into his mind, passing beneath his skin and emerging in a world newly made. For I knew that Cowell had written that country as I knew it; or else he had

45

sprung from the dark loins of its twisted gullies and when I entered his cabin and read there, I read to find him. Was that why I wanted to enter that country with Cowell at my side, to follow where he led through its valleys of green sound and speak, through him, with its native chiefs? That country needed to be spoken for, and if I wanted to hear it speak then it would speak for me with Cowell's voice: a young sound, yet one that bore an ancient wisdom, as if it were a piece of furniture, calm and precise, that, although ingeniously designed, had not forsaken the agedness of the tree.

One day I saw the figure of a man bathing in the river far below me. I stood on the forested cliff-top and watched that man's naked body, white and shining in the cold sunlight, as he moved himself to some ghost in the river or some native spirit. Immersed in that solitary act, I'm sure he would never have seen me where I stood, thirty feet above the water while he lay within its green blanket, bringing himself to come, lying inside his river, inside the body of his imaginary lover. When he emerged from the river he stood on its bank, a white god newly born, letting his skin dry in the clean cold sunlight. I thought of the children that would be born of that man and the river. Who would step from those waters in years to come? Who would pan those river silts for their gold? After he'd left I moved down the face of the gully to stand in the cold water and cool my ankles in the watery bed he'd made there. Eventually I wandered down the stream, slowly walking with the gentle flow of the water.

When I'd moved fifty yards downstream I discovered the body of a dead man, lodged in the branches of a sunken log below the surface of the water. Spread out, face-down, his dark hair and white hands moved in the gentle current, a green underwater breeze. He wore no clothing. His skin was white. Though I wondered who he was, I would not reach out and roll his body over. I would not look on his face.

When I found those words a cool wave of shock passed through me. Though I could not be certain, I was sure that Cowell must have watched me from a distance as I'd walked and lain naked in the native rivers. And as I read it was as if I had been the one violated, even though it was I who had stolen into Cowell's cabin and searched his private journal. I never told him that I had read what he had written there, nor did I ever ask him if he had watched me as I bathed. I never found out if he knew that I had read his words, the words where I'd been painted as a character in his journal, where I lay naked in the private room of his thoughts. But I felt a curious thing when I read those passages. For although I thought it had been me they'd described, though they'd been my actions, my private desires which Cowell had seen acted out in a moment when I had been certain that I was alone and unobserved, it was him I imagined in my place. His body, not mine, was the hinge of description made from the pile of words on the page. It was his naked white body I imagined bathing in the river below me. His were the hips I saw submerged in the water of a river, its green hands around his waist and thighs arousing him to hardness. It was his mind where

47

desire flowered while he thought of a woman's touch at the base of his spine. It was his pleasure when I came into that open water.

And if, as I read those words, it had been Cowell I'd seen lying naked in that water, if it had been Cowell who rose from his river bed a newborn god and walked away from me having spent himself there, then it was I who had wandered in his place, along the way he'd chosen down that wide green water, following the stream of seed to find the naked corpse of a white man caught in the underwater branches of a fallen log. It was I who'd seen and been reminded of a medieval machine of war in the sodden rotting arms of a massive trunk of native tree. I who'd decided against rolling that man over and looking into his dead face and I who'd wondered whether a white man had ever bathed in those green and freezing waters. I who had decided at that moment to stay my hand forever. Not merely to turn away, but to stand there always: always in the water, always wanting to reach out and lay my fingers, my palm, upon the waxy skin of the underwater man, to feel his once human flesh, flesh now dead but not decaying. It was I who was caught in that moment but helpless to act within it.

In later years I would often think of myself there, still standing in that river calmly flowing, not a muscle moving but watching the dead man's arms under water while they waved gently, forever.

In time my crimes were discovered. I was caught committing them. It was my habit to remain in Cowell's cabin long after I'd read from his diaries, and he came upon me late one afternoon as I stood with his book open in my hands. When he found me I was as docile and daydreaming as a steer standing mid-stream, having quenched its thirst; I made neither a sound of protest nor a word of defence but stood there dumbly while Cowell regarded me from the small doorway. He watched me; I watched him watching me. Then he spoke quietly as he stepped into the room and went among his things: 'Yes. I thought it was you. Your third visit. Maybe your fourth?' Then he looked at me and I asked him how he'd known that I'd been there before. He pointed to the treasure box on the floor at my feet and said, not unkindly, 'Yours are the worst knots on the ship.' I think he smiled. I told him I wanted to take nothing from his cabin. I told him I was no thief. He laughed and said that no, he didn't think I was a thief. He said I was the ship's cat, with a curiosity that led me around corners. 'I have been watching you. I have seen you walking. Far inland and all alone,' he said to me. My heart surged. He looked straight into me with his clear ageless eyes and said, 'This country is getting to you.'

'Yes,' I said.

--------------------------◀

Let me tell you about their Great Chief.

Cowell's voice in the dim light of the small oil lamp of his cabin. A calm sea out there, in the late evening, in the black shadow of the planet. This tiny room an ochre box in our wooden cradle, a speck floating upon it.

Let me tell you about their Great Chief. He was born the same year that Cook first sailed here, the same year that Cook first spied and landed on these islands and named, after himself, the straits that lay between them. That was sixty years ago. At that time most natives still lived and died never having seen the skin of a white man. So he was born, then, this Great Chief, this Wolf that the natives call Te Rop'raha, among the last people in the world to die without ever having looked into European eyes. And if you ever look into the Wolf's face, remember that when those clear and fearsome eyes looked out from the face of a child they looked into the eyes of old men to whom Europe herself was unknown, unimaginable. Now he is an old man sitting on the edge of an old world, Te Rop'raha. Born among the last of the natives to live beyond the gaze of Europe; living among the first to feel English hands reaching after their clear New Zealand air. Isn't it true that we always value the first and the last among people?

Two days ago we sailed past the wide bay of his ancient tribal homeland; I could have pointed out the pale outline of the hills far inland where, as a young man, a young leader of war, he spilled the blood of his neighbours. Those low gentle hills were where his trail of blood began, before he moved south through the ribcage of the island, tearing its heart to shreds as he went. We could have put ashore and walked upon an earth still bearing the scars he made there.

For the last thirty years ships from England and Europe have sailed this stretch of water, sailing these sea-roads north and south but never landing, so dangerous and war-torn were these western provinces. Now the country here is safer; now there are traders with stations along these bays. Ten years ago, when the sea-traffic passed up and down its ocean highway without any thought of landing, the natives, watching from the shore, assumed those ships were sailed by spirits: by the 'Wara-kee', the white-skinned gods of the ocean. But although we were goblins to them, mysterious and magical, in the years that we first appeared over the horizons of their seas we were not unknown to them: they already had names for us. Before our grandfathers first dreamed of these sea-green fields, these whale-roads, the New Zealanders told stories about white men. Before we'd even seen their savage islands and given them names of our own, they knew we sailed beyond the edges of their private green world. There are songs here, hundreds of years old, whose words describe the tall wooden ships of Europeans.

I smiled at Cowell's fancies. But he went on.

In this country the buried past can be carried upon a shoulder. The thread of a single song can carry the names of forty generations. Chants bearing the names of forty chiefs can carry the singer across oceans and years, thousands of miles back towards a homeland that has long since passed out of living memory and into the spoken machine of myth. The great chieftains of New Zealand claim their ancestry from legendary canoes. In this way the Wolf is descended from Ty-nui, one of the earliest canoes to have steered or drifted to these islands, one of the great vessels to come out of the Pacific, bringing with it the first people and native dogs and sweet potatoes. The Wolf has a name that calls back to a history so ancient that it will be sung as long as there are voices to carry such myths. Even here, in the small cabins of English merchant brigs, strange names can be carried and passed forward on the backs of stories. And what names does the Wolf carry for himself? Let me tell you about names.

Cowell paused to drink.

When he was a baby his father was killed in battle and the body eaten by the leader of an enemy tribe. Having made a feast of the father, this savage swore to kill and eat the young son of his slain and devoured enemy. He promised that the child would be roasted and made into a relish for the tasty thick-leafed convolvulus which grew on the sandy banks of the river near the sea. The boy's tribe was incensed. They swore an oath to protect the child of their dead chief, and defiantly renamed the boy after the river plant of their enemy's boast. So the boy who had been known as 'The Trickster', named after a god, was now called 'The Convolvulus Leaf', 'Te Rop'raha'.

Ah, I thought to myself, Convolvulus . . . do not forget his name!

Te Rop'raha. Such a gentle sounding name for a boy baptised with the blood of his own father. But as he became older he became bloodthirsty. He became a storm. And in a country with no shortage of slaughter-cruel warrior chiefs, Te Rop'raha became the most slaughter-cruel, feeding on the savagery of war like a vulture falling upon a

52

carcass, making a cloud of flies in the air over the body of these bloody islands.

Ruthless Te Rop'raha, cunning beyond all imagining. And yet when he drove his people into war, he then delivered them from death, leading them through the heart of the country to a new home in the south: to this island, Entry, which we sail towards. To the safety of those beaches, Te Rop'raha led them, on a raft of war through seas of harvests he steered them. He found a way through all the spears of the Northern Island, a trail hidden in the thickness of native forests, carving paths which had never been found and following them to the small dark island where he sits now like an eagle on the nest, a savage king on a dark throne. Kopitee, the New Zealanders call this island, meaning 'precipitous'. It is a good name, for its sheer western side plunges hundreds of feet into the sea where it sits, impregnable, as fast as a fortress. It will never be taken from his iron grasp.

On our maps it is called Entry, for it lies at the edge of Cook's Straits and stares clean through that belt of water, a long look south along the Middle Island's eastern side. The earliest European captains to these islands knew that anyone who held this tiny island would control all traffic to the Middle Island, that vast thigh of the earth that stretches for hundreds of miles into the south towards the frozen bottom of the world. So now Te Rop'raha's hands lie stretched over the water in two directions: one hand rests on the bottom of the Northern Island, the island on which he was born, while the other has already begun to creep south, even now grasping the top of the Middle Island by the scruff of its neck. He wants that island, he would swallow it whole. He has circled it and knows its weight. And although these islands are larger than Britain he knows their exact shape, he has seen their every harbour, their every bared knee and elbow of rocky shore. His great canoes of war have eyed these coasts like carrion fowl and he will not rest till his name is heard in every corner of the country like a whispering terror on the wind, a spirit biting the ear and a shot of poison ferried to the heart.

His name is an echo in even the steepest and emptiest of places, carried into the lost valleys that have never been spoken by a human voice, a soul in the far south-western corner of this country where the land wears a cloak of forest so dark and dense that the New Zealanders themselves have never set foot beneath it, even though the foot of some forgotten sailor made the first human shape in the sand of this country a thousand years ago. Can you imagine that moment when the first human foot was flung over the side of a tattered ocean-going canoe, when the first sole was plunged into the sand of a beach somewhere at the edge of this Northern Island? Imagine the vast history of that beach, untroubled by anything human since the earth was first born. Imagine the weight of the ages lapping on its sands. How can we grasp the single moment that changed the history of these islands forever? We can only imagine the foot, brown and bare, muscles calloused and sculpted by the years of its labour, the months of its travel. Stowed like a fishing net, or a primitive harpoon, tucked beneath the body of a sailor for days on end when it knew only the boards of a canoe moving upon the shifting weight of the ocean, when it felt only the steady rise and fall of a wooden floor, in this way measuring the miles it travelled and the breathing of the blue planet beneath it. Perhaps in the soft flesh underneath the toenails it carried traces of Tahitian sands, gritted like memory deep within itself, and perhaps it bore its knowledge of different islands across the sea like a verse or a necklace. For it must have been the foot of a sailor who knew the paths of the southern ocean like he knew songs made of strings of names. How many shores had he stepped upon as he navigated his way over the smooth blue curves of the planet to come at last to these islands, these curling columns of smoke above the enormous white anchor of the earth? Imagine this foot, travelling like a piece of driftwood carried over the planet's great southern oceans and carrying a person through a life, steering and following him through a history, whole and contained, from his first steps as a small child in a village whose name is now forgotten, to this fraction of time, this moment when it stepped onto the fringe of this crust of the earth that had drifted alone since the beginning. When it split the story of these islands in two. Reach for that quiet and holy moment when there was no before and no after: the seconds of history when the country's first footprint was made, when a human foot was first pressed into the wet grains of sand to set off an avalanche of human history. Who was that man, exhausted and starving, the first brown-skinned child of a new earth, who first collapsed onto the sandy golden edge of these plentiful green islands, who lay on the cradle of a strange beach and opened his eyes to find he had become the father of a country yet to be named?

But neither he nor any of his children down the years ever wandered into those far-southern forests treacherous-dark and steepest green, still growing like a memory of the land from before the time, centuries ago, when the first people stepped here. In those forests there might still walk the last remnants of a race of giant birds never seen by white men. Huge flightless things, more like giraffes than birds that have passed out of living memory, preserved only in the dry caves of native stories. They have disappeared like the eagles which used to fly down from the mountains, blackening the dusk air with the beating of their terrible wings, tearing apart with their screams the cold evenings when they poured into valleys to carry off men and women, children by the pair. Those birds came from heaven like avenging angels. I thought they could only have been terrors told in stories until a day when I wandered into the deep places of this country and came to the palaces of limestone where the floor is covered with the bones of enormous birds. In one shallow chamber I counted over two dozen talons spread wider than my outstretched hand, the claws sharper than shark-tooth, the legs strong enough to carry a man by the shoulders. Those eagles flew from the land long ago but, before they disappeared, men feared them as they now fear Te Rop'raha. So he is the last eagle in a land where the mightiest of all eagles have vanished. He is the Great Wolf in a land that has never known wolves.

He is a storm and he is the weather of the country, a

56

silver flood that falls from the darkened sky. He is the white edge of a cloud whose undersides stretch miles away into grey-black shadow. He is this cloud made in the shape of a gull's wing, its high edge blown and gilded with sunlight. He is the raft this cloud makes over the space of the earth. He is this vast green country, seen laid out from a great height. He is the birds. He is every speck of dust afloat in the air, gathered together and hurled with a force. He is a mountain and he is the hidden path up its side. He is the river and he is in the river, and he lies there asleep in the dreams of men. He is a convolvulus growing near the waters flowing over the green-stone lying, made and waiting for his greedy gathering. He is the shiver of sharks following this ship. He is a shark and he is the dark and silent water it swims through, a creature of the deep. He marries chieftains' daughters. He is the hot smell of battle and he is the victory of a battle-feast. He is the carved canoes of war that charge like cattle beasts. He is the birds. He is the sky. He is a storm on the wing.

We are sailing towards him and he is coming. He is waiting for us for he knows about this little ship treading the whale-road towards his island. He knows we've come to trade. He knows the traffic as he knows our road.

Cowell drained his whisky and set his glass down.

He is waiting.

He is coming.

IV.

Anchors, a Desert

Cowell's cabin became a habit of the late evenings. I
entered it each night after ten o'clock. I knew its rules of
disclosure as I knew my own thirst and hunger for the
stories it contained. It was a cabin which overflowed with
stories told through rum and whisky. The second night
we met there we were joined by Richardson, the third by
the two Georges: Wall and Brown. Each night Cowell's
cabin housed more listeners. Then there were rumours.
Murmurings of the mysterious evenings of entertainment
to be had in Cowell's quarters spread like wildfire through
the ship. Each man onboard sought the spark of their
origin, followed the smoke of whispers.

   As our number increased we began to drink more of
the ship's rum, the rum we'd brought and kept aside for
trade. We told ourselves that the natives hadn't properly
developed a taste for the grog. Muskets and razors, tobacco
and blankets – that was their preferred currency. And

besides, the casks took up so much room beneath deck. Later we would need that space for the tons of native flax we envisaged carrying under our return sail. We were doing the ship a service, Cowell told us. We were happily swayed to apply ourselves in earnest to the ship's duty.

On the fourth day the captain, Stewart, sent Clementson to marshal our thirsts. He opened the small doorway and barked in at us huddled inside. He said the captain knew we'd been stealing the rum from the hold. He said he heard us pissing it over the side of the boat in the middle of the night. And then he sneered and said that for all he cared we could drink till we fell overboard and drowned, one by one, forgotten in the heathen sea. But then he stepped closer to us and eyed Cowell with an open menace.

'Mister Cowell,' he said, 'if we're short of rum when we come to trade then I'll cut off your balls and feed them to the savages of Entry before your very eyes.'

Clementson hung there for a moment in the silence he'd created then turned and stomped out. When he'd left, Cowell raised his mug and toasted him.

Other, distinct, rumours circulated. The ship's tobacco was running low. Gold had been found. There was a mutiny in the offing and each night a meeting of conspirators took place in the supercargo's cabin. These stories drifted as harmless as vapours in the night-air over the sea, ignored by the captain and his chief mate. Then came a rumour of a native woman kept tied up in Cowell's bunk. Clementson stormed back in, late one night and without warning. He would not leave until he was satisfied that none of the

crew was keeping, in secret, the native cunt which for him
had remained sadly unattained. He left empty-handed
but the rumour persisted; his visit had only deepened the
suspicions of others onboard. One by one each man came
to see for himself if there was a ship's whore. Eventually
they all saw there was no woman. Although some were
dismayed, the curious stayed to hear Cowell's stories and
drank with us to the strength they desired. Not seven-
water grog, but half and half rum, or whisky without the
thread. Cowell thought Clementson an empty threat. We
all followed where Cowell led.

So the little cabin was alight in the evenings, a small
society of sailors in thrall to the exploits of Te Rop'raha,
that most fearsome of natives with whom we desired to
trade in a matter of days. From then on it was clear to us
we were sailing under Cowell. We were sailing under the
bard of the Wolf.

His voice made green worlds.

Have you walked through these rooms
of valleyed forest?

Have green slanting vines,
or black trunks of palm, scaled as though carved,
their thin leaves of lines,
ever stopped you,

given you pause to consider,

and remember,
on the wallpaper of drawing rooms at home,
fleur-de-lis?

Have you heard the bells of the dawn
chorus in cathedral trees?

Those bells wear cloaks of feathers.

Harsher
and more melodious
than any English variety,
the colours of the forest
and songs sleek
upon them.

But underneath
a pair of green wings
sudden flashes of orange insignia.

Splashes
of a red saddle
across a black feathered back.

The bluest sky carried in wattles
beneath a beak of gun-metal grey.
That bird carrying his tiny buckets of sky,
of river.

Then his call, strange
beyond the description of any
language
or the beauty of any
music.

Ducks of Paradise flying in pairs through the calm grey
of the morning. In the final half hour before dawn, in the
chilled quietness of the world. The stilled surface of a lake
while it waited for the sun. An early world with its breath
deeply held. And Te Rop'raha, seen from a distance, over
the far reach of glass, cold in the morning, the black shape
of a man in a canoe rowing to an island in the middle of
the lake to shoot the birds there for eating. He landed on
that island in the lake and the sun rose and the shots of
his gun split the morning in two. Here was the lord of the
dawn and the lord of morning shooting. Here was the lord
of the hunt, Herne, the spirit of the forest lakes. When Te
Rop'raha saw still water he read a gesture, a hand signal
from the native gods: Go to that island and make sport of
the birds that nest there. Here is a sign, here is a road. Here
is a place of good hunting. Here is a gift of birds.

Beside me the Watcher sat slumped in his seat. His eyes
were closed and I thought he had fallen asleep. 'A gift of
birds,' he repeated slowly, the voice as relaxed as the hands
of a sleeping man, the eyes still gently shut. 'A gift of birds.'

It is said that at the heart of the Northern Island there lies a vast desert. According to the stories this is a land of volcanoes which freezes over in the winter months. No white man has ever been there. It is said that the Wolf once ran the length of this high plain of broken earth all alone.

Te Rop'raha made his great desert crossing when he was a young man, a warrior-pup stumbling into a history of disputed territories. He appeared at the edges of wars, decades old, waged over the ownership of fertile grounds. How should I describe for you the land that this was? This was a land where storehouses were made to contain food and proclaim the wealth of certain tribes, made to stand like cairns where the thickness of forests lapped against the calm fields of crops. Each building was made to mark boundaries of influence upon the land. Effigies of chiefs were made to stand and watch over certain gullies, like totems beside ancestral rivers. In this country all spirituality was geological. Here, religion dwelt in the mountainsides. Trade and politics were the grasses that grew on them, whose seeds were carried by mountain breezes.

To the young Wolf, every carving he passed on his far roaming was a gesture and a challenge. The carved posts of houses were made to be burned down, reduced to heavy piles of black ashes and turned to mud beneath the weight of grey winter rains. A row of sweet potatoes, sown in the earth, was planted to be stolen. Strange women were to be lain against beneath blankets in cold weather, and after the warmth of their bodies had been taken from them, left with loathsome thoughts, tears and hunger. Whenever the Wolf saw a strange chief he wanted to tear out his eyes and bury his cock inside the blind man's wife.

The Wolf did not walk over the land but stalked it in a rage.

When he was barely twenty years old he led a hundred and forty of his men into far northern territories, stalking an enemy two hundred-strong as it moved through the rainforest, a pack animal laden with goods acquired in trade. The Wolf tracked them as they wandered towards their home over the ways of high mountains. And though this enemy travelled in a war-party, Te Rop'raha knew the days of rain were a weapon to be fashioned against them. For tribes who had traded for mats and gourds and dried fishes from the sea could only move slowly across those wet mountain trails. When night fell in the dense and freezing ranges of the interior he attacked them. Swinging out of the trees his ferocious band slaughtered them by the dozen and in the confusion of storm-tossed darkness all men were scattered so friends and enemies could not tell each other apart. Through black rain the Wolf ran for safety. For days he ran, aimlessly descending the steep mountain ranges till the black, wet trunks and branches of sinister trees turned to hands of thorny scrub reaching out of the ground whose muddy trails turned to rocks beneath his bare feet. For days he ran, his feet bleeding and torn, eating the bodies of dead birds he found in rivers. When he turned his face to the thin cloak of cold wind at his back he knew the enemy had come after him.

He turned and dived into the desert, into a lake of blasted earth. He ran like a swimmer of the dead country that lay all around him. He ran through the desert air swiftly as a hunted hare.

For days the enemy behind stalked him across the hostile plains, expecting his worn out figure to appear ahead of them over the next desert ridge, or the next, for they thought they were tracking a delirious animal in the final stages of life, terrified and tiring, a man staggering like a wounded ox. In the frozen mornings they expected to find his desert corpse freshly fallen in the night, still warm enough to take meat from. They thought of the soup they would make from his brains, the cooked flesh they would gnaw from his charred bones. His green eyes and how they would be swallowed. But through the days and nights he ran invisible ahead of them. Only the brightly hanging moon saw him as he ran the high desert plain under the southern ceiling of the world. The cross, known to the ancient Athenians, pointed his way among the strange stars spread across that blue-black sky of moon. Only the snow-covered sides of volcanoes, carrying the moonlight, were visible about him as he ran. Only the swiftest of desert wolves was Te Rop'raha, sure-footed in the dark, skipping over death. For this is no desert of folding yellow sand drifting on curtains of winds, but a plain of volcanic dust and rocks, burnt black, whose backs break into crevices large enough that a man could fall into their cavernous depths, hidden in shadow, and die of thirst before he could find and climb his way out. Whose cracks make traps of rocky teeth in the land small enough to break a human ankle. A man maimed in this way may crawl for days before perishing through some lack or other on that desert floor, lying in the wind and the sun, the rain and the snow. And though this volcanic desert lies frozen in winter, it is a monster whose jaws never close. And the men hunting the Wolf grew afraid of him. 'Who is this young warrior chief, worn out from battle, tired and alone, running this desert ahead of us without perishing?' they asked themselves. 'What shape has he taken?' they asked each other. And in the freezing evenings they saw a single desert hawk, miles high, wheeling around their position in a wide arc. They said that it was Te Rop'raha taken to the air to see where they lay for the night and they hid from him. But while they rested he ran on through the night, watching his shadow beside him, using its angle to keep direction, the shape moving like dark water over rocks. He prayed to the goddess of the moon.

And as he ran he chanted. I am dead I am alive I am dead I am alive.

A chant that carried him across the desert.

I am dead I am alive I am dead I am alive.

The air tasted of Spring. We had brought the months across the ocean with us, a string of days from February to September, a kite-tail in the ocean winds, but as we sailed the character within them had been changed. When we left England February had been the last cold stone of winter, a wide step slowly warming itself in the sun. Here it was the wooden door closing shut on a tired summer, swung by the weight of a tilting earth. The September we knew had been the month of Sunday afternoons, of calm nostalgic autumns. A cathedral of red leaves and the heavy smoke of the first fires. But here it was a corridor of new light and wild breezes.

With these strange new months came other confusions. As we sailed around the world we had misplaced the date. We knew it lay crouched near the end of September, though when we agreed it was the thirtieth Richardson remembered that it was still the evening of the twenty-ninth in England. 'My mother's birthday,' he murmured, and so as we looked at the fierce new sun rising warm over the wild morning we thought of the cold light that we imagined it had left in the last hours of a darkening British sky. A fading sunset in our minds a whole world away from the bright morning of this strange green country, new to us and ancient. The sun was brighter here. Its light was wilder and younger, its heat more savage. The legends told in these islands spoke of men who had gone to war against it, for the New Zealand sun was a mischievous god. They had caught him in enchanted ropes of woven flax and tamed him, beating him with a weapon made of magic jawbone. Then they had released him into the sky, ordering him to wander across it more slowly.

We saw that everywhere around the world even the sun could be made to fit the shape of local mythology. Yet even here, we heard the echoes of older, northern gods. Cowell told us the New Zealanders called the sun Ra, as the ancient Egyptians had. We wondered how that name could have travelled around the world. Had it drifted on the same ocean currents we trod? Had it been blown like a bird in a storm, across hundreds of miles of windy seas? Or had it been carried in a hold, stowed as vitally as provisions and warm mats, fish hooks and seeds?

We learned other words, new names. 'Kooma-ra' meant sweet potato. Cowell told us this word was the same across all Pacific Islands, had been found as far east as South America. The New Zealanders, it was said, carried maps of the ocean currents within them, just as they had named all the southern stars over their heads. So they had marked their ocean highways. Where the Greeks had seen a cross in the sky, the New Zealanders had found and named an anchor.

*

*

*

*

Across the ship men scrubbing her decks in the mornings could be heard reciting the native names for sweet potatoes and anchors.

Kooma-ra Te Punga. Kooma-ra Te Punga.

What would have seemed like nonsense to the natives

became a chant to us. 'Kooma-Ra Te Punga!' chorused together while raising a sail in a team of men. Or 'koomara te punga,' a quiet private prayer, its soft thumps under the breath as one walked alone upon the deserted shore in the afternoons.

We reduced the syllables to a rhythm of sounds. We lost sight of what they were supposed to mean when spoken as words. We confused potatoes for anchors, anchors for potatoes.

One morning a small group of us went ashore to trade blankets for vegetables with a tribe of New Zealanders known to live a mile or so inland. We knew this tribe for they had supplied us before. Cowell had slept among them in their village. On the beach Evans insisted on going on alone. 'These natives are no bother,' he said. He was a big ginger man and if he said he was going alone then he was going alone. Brown looked at Cowell and Cowell looked the other way. The captain and chief mate were back aboard the brig out in the bay. Evans heaved the blankets over his shoulder and tramped off alone.

He returned, hours later, with a native anchor. When our dumbfounded stares gave way to curses and insults he said quickly that he had forgotten the word for potato, that he must have had it confused with the word for anchor. Later, on board the *Elizabeth*, I watched as Evans knelt down and ran his hands over the rounded sides of his luminous dark rock, not large but heavy, perhaps made to contain the spirit of a native deity. It sat on the deck like a pouch, a small shapely hole at the top where a rope of native flax could be tied. I saw the concentrated pride in

Evans's clear blue eyes, strong as the sky, his appreciation for its seaman's craftsmanship, its sculptural beauty. When his wide freckled hands touched that sea-stone I saw him feel the weight of history it contained. 'A beautiful thing,' he muttered to himself. 'A beautiful thing and a thing well made. Yes, a beauty all right,' he spoke softly to himself. I wondered if he'd known the word for sweet potato all along and if he'd gone alone to the New Zealanders with only that anchor in mind, a native treasure seen and lovingly eyed on some previous trip ashore.

It lay above deck overnight.

When we woke in the morning we saw that someone among the crew had risen soundlessly in the night, passed up to the level of the deck and crudely hacked sharp letters into the side of Evans's anchor. 'COO MA RA,' carved in the white colour of the stone where it had been scratched by a flint. An attempt at the word for potato turned into an insult and a prank. Men waited for Evans nervously, anticipating the thunderous moment when he made the discovery for himself. But the fateful moment, when it came, came quietly. There was no fury or bellowing. There was no cursing or swearing, no oath to find the perpetrator and no promise to string him up by his balls. There was only the forlorn figure of Evans standing helplessly before his spoiled treasure, his head cocked to one side, the countenance of a small boy caught in the body of a wounded bull, hypnotised by the ugly Roman letters adorning his prize of New Zealand stone. There is something about seeing a big man defeated that I cannot bear. I went to him and spoke quietly at his side. I said we would find out who had done this thing. Without turning his eyes upon me or shifting the furrow from his brow Evans said no, we did not need to find the man. I did not understand him but I let him have his way. Quietly and firmly he refused my help as he lifted the anchor and carried it below deck and into the hold.

Evans did not say a word to a single man all day. A mood hung over the ship, as heavy and charged as thunder clouds, a storm that would neither break nor blow away. In the evening we ate a forsaken broth. The men complained. Even the natives ate pork, they said. Even the savages had potatoes. And at the mention of potatoes the table fell silent. Only Evans flickered. He rose up and roared half in laughter, 'Shove it up your arse!' and hurled a potato at Brown, for at that moment he realised that he alone had been served stew with sweet potatoes while the rest of us had only a thin, meagre soup. Food rained down upon Evans, thrown by a horde of laughing men. The storm had broken. That night the men got drunk and sang songs together.

In Evans there was a determination to love every man upon the ship, our tribe upon the waves. He carried this love within him, a private code that steered him through paths of men. I wondered again if he had deliberately sought out the anchor of the New Zealanders and if it had been the reason he'd insisted on trading alone, without the company of others and away from the guidance of the trading master. And I wondered if when he saw the scratched words upon its side then he remembered the code he had carried within himself and betrayed: not forgotten, but wilfully cast aside. For when he gained that anchor he'd sold the faith of his own ship for the price of a blanket. And his refusal to find any man guilty was a measure of his own guilt. So the words scratched onto the side of his anchor were a message to Evans from whatever angel was watching him in those strange savage islands. He'd heard his angel speak in the words of a savage tongue, making relics of anchors and signs of potatoes.

We thought of the anchor in the sky, the southern cross, as Te Rop'raha's cross, for it had been the constellation that had guided the Wolf on his desert run. We thought of it as the eye of Te Rop'raha looking down on us. We thought of it as a giant sign in the sky pointing us to Kopitee. It was the footprint of the island and it was the island's airborne soul making Entry into a ghost that hovered above us. It was easy for us to imagine the tribes in this country hiding from hawks wheeling overhead for fear of being seen by a magical enemy. Everything had sinister eyes in this country, everything had a spirit climbing within it. The native parrots were inquisitive and intelligent. They must have been people at one time. Everything was alive.

The stories here grew like trees, spreading roots underground as they stretched their high branches and leaves overhead. And as they crowded the landscape, growing for thousands of years like a green blanket, like a black twisted cage, they carried a memory of the seeds they'd been in the beginning though they'd grown and no longer looked like seeds. They could no longer be held in the palm of a human hand. They were larger than us, the stories of these islands. We could not contain them, though we built our ships to carry pieces of them, their anchors, their sons' heads, their vegetables.

Their stories, such as we found them, began to live in us. They left their footprints in the soil of our souls. They had a foothold there. They left their little seeds in our care, and we found that we could not leave behind the story of the Wolf running alone through the frozen desert, the stars and moon above him as he ran, surrounded by the tremendous volcanoes not yet grazed by a white man's eye, his heels flicking like the tails of two bolting rabbits in the night. We'd left him running. We had to know what had happened, how far he'd run.

'The Great Wolf . . .' said Wall quietly. 'Did they catch him?'

'Ah . . . listen . . .'

We leaned forward in the dark to catch the pieces of story as they were flung to us.

*

On the fifth morning the sea of desert broke all around him. He stood amid the crashing waves of sudden greenery, their festival of colour. He walked between the walls of high grasses. He waded the mountain tussocks and cantered over unexpected gentle hillsides. He passed like a shadow into the cool pools of shadow, beneath the thickets of immense native beeches that stood on the flanks of foothills, trees like cattle resting in the heat of the middle of the day. Dazzled by sunlight, weariness and hunger, he wondered if he had wandered into paradise. He thought he'd died and arrived in an empty heaven.

*

The Wolf left a trail of bloody footprints as he walked through the grass. When he turned and saw the blood-soaked ground, its green and brown blades bent and broken, he saw that the earth in heaven bled red human blood.

*

He entered a silent village, a collection of dark houses whose angled wings of roofs were not sleeping but emptied of their warrior spirits. He fell to the dusty earth. When he lifted his head he looked into the eyes of a naked boy, not five years old, standing and watching him.

'Where are your men?' cried Te Rop'raha, but the child did not answer.

Women with long dark hair and tattoos of moon carved black and green into their lips, into the curved bones of their chins, emerged slowly from their thatched huts and houses and circled him where he lay. 'Where are your men?' asked Te Rop'raha again, weakly, but the strange women did not answer and Te Rop'raha thought he'd died again. 'I died and walked into the arms of heaven. When I entered heaven I died and fell again.' Then the world turned black around him.

*

When he woke he woke in a glove of darkness, in the mustiness of the earth, held in the smell of sweet potatoes.

The shapes of crosses came out slowly over his head. In time his eyes grew used to the darkness and he saw the crosses were patterns woven into the underside of a flaxen mat laid across the mouth of the pit high above him. Cast into the opened ground of a food chamber hollowed from the earth, Te Rop'raha the Wolf saw that he had been made a prisoner.

Neither alive nor dead or dying; time's slow paw rested in the earth.

*

There was a woman's voice he did not know.

'Te Rop'raha came to this village. We hid from him and heard him passing like the wind between the walls of our houses. He shook our roofs over our trembling heads, but he did not find us. We heard the storm he made but his hands of wind and rain did not touch our soft pumice skins. When the earth was still again, empty of his demon, we crept from our huts into the clean air. When we looked into the distance we saw him moving against the low eastern hills, a dark shape moving across the face of the earth like the shadow of a bird.'

Hidden in the ground below this voice speaking, in the small dark well beneath the woven stars, the Wolf thought, 'Who is this woman? Why does she lie?'

Thus he lay buried like a crocus bulb in the quiet, warm earth, in the safety of a womb, in the net of stars. And upon the ground the gentle voice of the woman spoke like the magnet of sun to a pale, soft stem pushing upwards through dark soil. Te Rop'raha thought of that woman standing above him, her legs astride the pit where he hid, the high archway into heaven they made. He thought of the warm, wet pocket inside her and hardened. He would break the surface of the earth and pluck her like a ripe, soft pear. He would eat her like a piece of fruit.

He pushed against the roof of his dark world and made a small tear in the ground, a gentle wave, a ripple where he had lifted the edge of the mat from the surface of the earth. Afternoon sunlight spilled in, sucked like a tide, and the Wolf peered out across the country of low orange light. He saw a forest of dark shapes moving like liquid within it, the dark swaying trees of men, hundreds gathered, their hairy legs and thick trunks surrounding him where he stood, still hidden in the ground, standing upright in his chamber of the earth. In his limbs the hardness of desire became cold water flowing thinly through his veins and his heart beat like a rabbit's when it was caught in a trap. He knew these men. He had heard their voices before, carried behind him on the drafts of frozen desert air as he'd run those high broken ridges. He had inhaled them, their ghost of sound, like smoke in icy air taken deep inside his cold and gasping lungs.

Te Rop'raha fell back to the deep floor of the hole in the earth. He did not know if it was a cage or a well he lay within, if it was a trap made of the earth or a cloak of safety wrapped about him.

'Where are your men?'
'Where are your men?'

In the stories of New Zealand, a village empty of men
meant one had died and found heaven's houses, the quiet
dwellings of its virgin-witches. Or one had not died, but
wandered the earth of shaky green isles and found a
village from which a war-party had left to roam the land
with spears. Like baited traps these villages sat, steel teeth
prised apart and waiting for an unlucky animal to wander
in. Such an animal was the Wolf. He lay in the earth
underneath a village whose spear-winds had blown home.
So those jaws had closed upon his body, a morsel of meat
they did not know was there.

*

Time passed in the earth. Upon the earth quietness fell.

The woman appeared in the open mouth of sky above
him – in the light of the late afternoon her face was the
sun. Her dark hair fell towards him – she was a brown
young willow bending low over the dark edge of a green
forest pool. Here was the wife of his enemy. He climbed
towards her and rose into the quietness of a village once
more empty of men, as if a village submerged in a myth or
beneath the sea.

'You're the colour of a witch,' Te Rop'raha told her. 'If
you're no witch you'll feed me potatoes and cress.'

And so she led him across the ground of purple shadows to a chiefly hut. After he'd eaten there he lay with her, coming inside her in the bed of his enemy.

When Te Rop'raha left her he wandered to the edges of the village and looked beyond its spiked walls into the east.

'When we looked into the distance we saw him moving against the low eastern hills, a dark shape moving across the face of the earth like the shadow of a bird.'

He saw the army of his enemy there, moving like a shadow, following the invisible trail they'd been told he'd left behind. So he knew then that he'd not dreamed their voices when he'd lain like a carcass or a seed in the ground beneath the huts of their own village, but that they'd followed him there, only to be deceived by the words of their own women who sent them away to wander in the empty hills.

The sun fell behind him in clouds whose edges shone like steel. He climbed the ramparts and called out to the far host of his enemy, issuing a cry of thunder, chanting a challenge and a mockery, dancing and screaming, tearing the evening air like a hail of heaven's golden arrows. His enemies turned and saw the tiny silhouette against the sunset, a small leaping goblin defying them from the top of their own walls two miles away.

I was dead! I am alive! I was dead! I am alive!
Your woman with the long hair – she is the sun
that lay with me and saved me.

See how she shines! I stepped towards her. One more step
and I have escaped, although your ranks hold fast,
into the sun that shines!
It is done!

So spoke Te Rop'raha, the cannibal-poet. He leaped
from the wall and disappeared into the sun-setting
west, into history. Into the stories told in the cabins of
merchant brigs.

At the end
of an evening's stories
told in that cabin,
to slip that chain

I traded the swirl of savage armies
– the grit of savage war,
their landscapes ravaged within me –
for the quiet walk,

the anonymous waltz
across the ship's open deck
beneath the strange stars'
chandelier.

At night, if you were the only man awake, the only man
watching, you saw the land give up its secrets. Sometime in
late September we had moored in the afternoon, in heavy

cloud, a little way from shore. By midnight the thick stuff had cleared to reveal a black night on which no medallion of moon was pinned to drown the brightness of stars. I stood alone on the deck and looked over the short field of sea to where the monster of land lay, its long black shadow lying low in the water. Silent trees I could not see sat huddled upon its back. I imagined them looking back at me, I felt their dark regard. I imagined unsleeping birds to be perched in their branches like open eyes woven into the backs of black shaggy leaves.

And in the inky moonless depths of those shades I saw a sudden ghost. I strained to make out its shape but it slipped from the very grasp of my eyes, shimmering at the edges of my vision when I looked to either side. After a few moments I held it more firmly and saw it to be a glowing white sail in the sky high above the black raft of land in the sea. Though I had never seen an angel before, I thought of it as an angel watching over a land whose tangled forests of rain had never known angels. And then it came into quick hard focus, firm and real before me. I held the shape of its wing, its shoulder, and I saw it was a single mountain rising over the earth miles into the air, its snowy cap glowing faintly in the blackest of nights. I breathed in this vision, for I was sure I was looking upon one of the ghosts of Te Rop'raha's desert volcanoes.

In the morning the cloud had packed down again so the land was mostly hidden from us upon the ship. I stood staring at the edge of the shore, its black sand and green forest behind, but the cloud was so low that there was little more to be seen. Still I stared, trying to make out through the thick cloud the shape of the volcano I had seen the night before. A few of the men jeered to see me standing there mutely staring into the blanket of nothingness. They shook me from my reverie and I shuffled awkwardly on the deck, looking to the ground to see if there was some rope or other which I could pretend I had meant to coil. There was none, and I continued to look to the ground in embarrassment. A short minute later Cowell passed near me where I stood.

'The New Zealanders have a saying,' he said slowly. 'If you must bow your head do so only to a lofty mountain.' He walked away without another word.

A day later we saw that mountain far behind us rising out of the flat earth we'd sailed beside. A light blue peak against a bright blue sky. Men marvelled and wondered how they'd missed it when we'd sailed past its stretch of shore. I did not tell them I had seen it two nights previous, floating in the night like an iceberg over the black, black sea.

In New Zealand, Cowell said, all mountains were related. The coastal peak we'd seen was the distant brother of Te Rop'raha's desert volcanoes. The men who had not heard Cowell's stories in the evenings thought him mad. 'He thinks in shades of brown,' they murmured to themselves. 'He sleeps with them, and moves among them. One day he'll wake up with tattoos on half his face and a taste for human meat.' They eyed him with fear and respect and tangled, buried longings. But Cowell's mind shifted under my skin and I felt his grip tighten. For I had seen that mountain in the middle of the night and felt its shimmer as though it had been a ghost of the desert. His stories lived in me and opened me.

In the days before we made Entry I stood in the stern of the brig and looked through clear blue air to the distant coastal volcano behind us. I felt Cowell's hand on my back, underneath my jaw, turning me to face the islands we sailed. I breathed in that wild air and felt those island breezes coursing through me. I felt the pleasure of that country, a sexual desire for its high winds and sheer green valleys I knew to be cradled inside its borders of shining shores.

So we sailed the wild coasts of deep green forests and shiny black sand, their blue and white air brighter and clearer than any church windows we'd ever seen. The wild morning smell of them. We sailed down this coast, against the green arm of its conqueror, the Southern Napoleon. The country slipped past our prow and as the stretch of those green miles grew we asked ourselves how the Wolf had tamed them. How had one man – an outcast among savages – brought this land of steep and folding valleys to heel beneath his will?

Whenever we asked a question, Cowell was an anchor.

Many years before we sailed down that rocky green coast, the Wolf had fired his first musket after a battle fought and won there. In those days muskets were still rare, possessing a sacredness beyond battle. When a local chief handed Te Rop'raha a firearm in the ritual of peace-making the Wolf unloaded it into the air. A hole of sound was ripped open between his ears and he felt a crack in his chest like a snap in the earth. He felt the power of thunder at his fingertips and saw that the white god of smoke had made a black wound in the sky above him. He did not pass the musket back. This steel claw, he thought to himself. I could take an island with such claws. He swore to sow war and reap a harvest of muskets.

After the Wolf had escaped the desert, after he'd been hidden and released by the wives of his enemy, he roamed the heart of the Northern Island. He crawled down its spine. He sent a shiver down its back. Villages were razed, food was stolen. Heads were clubbed where they slept. People heard whispers of a monster abroad. They felt the far off sounding of thunder, as though a hillside had fallen away in the mountains and its faint echo had come to rest in their villages near the sea. The world shuddered in a breeze, a swarm of gentle earthquakes, and men said that a demi-god, savage and angry, walked in the hills.

In the mountains Te Rop'raha heard the rumours. They rose towards him like smoke through gentle rains.

He spent a year in the mountains with a troop of a hundred savages, hard young warriors with green eyes and scarred faces, attracted to the stories of a wild chief in the hills whose terror lit up the mountain ranges like lightning in dark afternoons. These men had left their tribes and wandered into the mountains, passing up the forest trails in ones and twos, drifting up those tracks like smoke passing through the camouflage of rain and mist till they found him. In this way, the remnants of Te Rop'raha's lost one hundred and forty returned to him. For a year they plundered the mountains, terrifying as pirates and playful as the carnivorous native parrots that nested there.

When the Wolf returned to his tribe, to his people and to his wide ancestral harbour in the west, he returned with a scattered and torn tail of mercenary warriors behind him. When the Wolf returned those villages fell silent. Their son had become a mountain terror. They watched him, their Convolvulus Leaf drifting back to them, carried down towards them on a shelf of mountain air, and they saw his warriors spread out behind him. They waited for him and they watched him silently while he re-entered the fortified village he had left a year before. There was no sound to greet him. They watched him without flinching while they waited for his leap, teeth bared and lethal. As he hopped forward his spear flicked the air like a tail then rested like a pointed paw. But when he stepped through those gates, between those high teeth of spiked wood and over the threshold of his ancestors, when his foot pressed upon the dusty collarbone of earth, he sent out their songs in the air before him. He stood in the arms of his silent tribe and chanted the names of his mountain and his river, his tribe's mountain and his tribe's river. He offered incantations as intimate as his warm breath upon the naked young body of a girl of the tribe promised in marriage. So the tribe knew he had returned to them as a son, no weapons concealed about him. He pointed to the mountains behind him, south and to the east, where he'd dwelt for a year, and told the old chiefs that those ranges were now tribal lands. As he spoke he swept the air slowly with his open hand and so it seemed to them that he spoke the words of creation, speaking of mountains and showing them mountains, passing to them the hills from the palm of his hand. He had brought them no gifts but that chain of ranges, their pale blue view against the horizon, made into a shawl and pulled about their shoulders.

Te Rop'raha was a savage who knew that the earth could be a sea, a skin of water carved by currents and breezes, but that the land could also be steered like a ship, pushed by winds, by the wills of men as they gusted upon it. When he saw mountains he saw a frozen wave holding up the air and held up by the air. He knew that when you gave a man a gift of mountainsides, you told him where he could stand, you told him where he could look.

In times of jagged peace the Wolf travelled through the island brokering war. He did not trust the calm space which hung over the land that was empty of unrest, for it was unstable, always about to be smashed. Better, he said, to shatter than be shattered. He despised the weakness of peace, for as long as there was an enemy there was an enemy to be destroyed. As long as there were tribes there were lands to be taken. These are islands of earthquakes. These are islands with many gods: gods like grasses that grow on hillsides, and gods like fires that sweep hillsides bare of grasses. There are gods like rocks cast from mountains into rivers, and gods like rivers whose carved arms through mountains are used as highways.

When he went out into the world around him he turned and said to the old chiefs of his home: 'It is easy to tear apart that which has never existed. That is your peace. The gods choose instead to shake the ground beneath our feet. Save the songs you sing; they are broken as easily as the necks of slaves are broken. I would choke on the bones of my enemy before I sing your songs of peace. I will rule over an island; over your island and all islands.'

Who Will Take My Place? When those words, spoken by a dying chief, were pushed like a canoe onto the clear and dusky air of an autumn night, they were left to drift, rudderless, for no one answered. A cool evening wind blew into the meeting house where he lay, through the open door from the blue twilight outside, chilling the bones and hearts of all who stood gathered around their fading king.

Who Will Take My Place? And though none answered, in the corner of the room there crouched a Wolf. Hidden in shadows and moving within shadows, he moved slowly towards the body of the old man who lay there like a holy savage knight, a tired barbarian king waiting for the doors to heaven to open. And the Wolf moved on the last steps of a long journey towards him. For within this fading body was hidden the totem of Te Rop'raha; these were his mother's people. He had returned to them the same night that its chiefly light lay dying. He held onto this sign.

The old man looked with the last glow of the world in his eyes towards the figure creeping towards his death-bed. His upraised arm made a weak, dead branch, his skin of crushed dried leaves lay cradled in the palm. The Wolf crept closer till the old man's curled paw rested on his head, a purse of riches held there in the gesture of a dying hand. Here was the alliance Te Rop'raha sought, extended in the manner of a gift. Now he had only to close his jaws around the soft body of this expiring chief, as gentle and brittle as a newborn calf. Gently his teeth sank in.

I Will Lead Them, he said.

A room of earthly witnesses and spirits crowded the room as the Great Wolf took the dead man's wife and became the general of his tribe. The Wolf wielded tribes like weapons.

So we sailed the wild coasts of deep green forests and shiny black sand. The country slipped past our prow in a stretch of green miles, bright blue days. When we looked to that shore we saw his dark country from the engaged distance of our brig. We looked to his tangled tree-clad hills across the safety of small miles of sea. We sailed and moved like a speck down his vast side, an invisible itch against him. We had not yet become a satellite held in the magnetism of his orbit. We sailed sometimes nearer to his coast, sometimes further from it. We thought we were our own planet on the waves. Sometimes we landed and nestled in his side. Sometimes we moved among the tribes that lived there, trading for small goods as we needed them with the men who paid him tribute, people who brought him food and flax and to whom he gave in return gifts of flints. Blankets. Some rum. For a year of sweet potatoes they could earn a musket or a barrel of powder. If we asked them for flax they shook their heads. They had none, they said. But we knew that they lied, or that they did not understand how they could answer any different. We knew that for them all the flax they'd dressed and scraped belonged already to the Wolf.

After we had traded with them – a musty blanket for ten barrels of potatoes, an old steel blade, twisted and nicked, for twelve sacks of fish – we moved back out to our distance of sea and sailed along his side again, crawling over the shallow ocean towards him in the south. He was our target, our goal, our desired, our end. We sailed towards him. We sailed for his island, his flax emporium, his dark heart of trade. And slowly, as we crept nearer to him, we felt him becoming the sun. We felt ourselves drawn to him. We should have seen that we were a fish on the end of his line, that we were being reeled towards him. But in those last days before we arrived at Entry we still felt as though we walked beside that island, that we held it by a leash, and although it led us like a dog and tugged on the lead we held, we thought we chose to hold it for in our minds we were still its power, we were still the mind that steered it. As we sailed down to Entry, to Kopitee the Precipitous Isle, we felt him like a weight at the end of ourselves, an anchor beneath our brig, a native rock below our English timbers.

But what was it we sailed towards? For though he drew us towards him, though he was the sun and we were a planet held and swung by his arms of light, we could not see his face. Blinded by the radiance of stories shining from him, his face remained dark and unknowable, outshone by the words we'd heard describing it, by the warmth of poetry that crept and sat upon our skins, holy as sunlight, wrought in his image though his was a visage we'd never seen.

We were in his waters.
We had fair sailing.
We were his traffic.

A few days before we reached Entry we saw, ahead of us
and a short way off shore, a small schooner. Kirkpatrick
recognised her. 'There's the *Waterloo*,' he said. We expected
to draw up beside her but Stewart said we would not stop
to speak with her. Men murmured among themselves.

Kirkpatrick frowned like a crestfallen child, for he knew
Guard, the captain of the *Waterloo*. To a man we'd all heard
stories of brave Jacky Guard, the whaler who'd lived on
these islands for years, for years surviving the annoyances
of the unfriendly natives. They'd burned down his house
but he'd built himself another. They'd ravaged the turnips
he'd planted and so he'd survived instead on the flesh and
blubber of beached whales. They'd plundered the stacks
of whale bone he had gathered to trade with passing
Europeans and he'd not been moved to anger, instead
calmly gathering more bone and hiding it more cleverly.
We knew all about brave Jacky Guard. He was as sternly
driven as the gale which, three years before, had forced him
ashore to live on the harsh coast while his ship lay broken,
his crew drowned or scattered. He could have taken
passage back to Sydney, for he had floundered on a well-
travelled shore, but he chose to stay. He would not leave
the country where God had wrecked him without taking
something from the heart and face of that country. He

turned down every offer of safe passage back to Australia and ranted instead to the traders of the riches that waited to be whaled in the bays of New Zealand.

Send ships and make stations! he'd ordered, this bearded madman in rags living in a hut all alone on the shore.

His words drifted back to New South Wales and into the ears of the new money there. He wrote letters and his letters were answered, their replies delivered to him by the most frequent of the friendly ships: the *Dragon*, the *Argus*. In a year more ships were sent from Sydney to build the whaling stations he had implored. A ship was sent for Guard: the *Waterloo*. He became her captain and started a whaling trade.

We sailed past them. The captain and Clementson stood at our prow watching in the direction of the little schooner and its fierce captain. Cowell stood with us watching Stewart and his mate. Kirkpatrick's excited chatter went on – Guard as tall as a tree, arms like fence posts, a shock of hair redder than all the flames of all the fires burning in hell. Cowell stood with his arms folded, his mind elsewhere, somewhere near the two figures standing at the front of the brig. And in that moment I saw the working of his mind, how his thoughts turned against his captain and his captain's mate. I saw it in a clear second. As we sailed past the *Waterloo* Stewart sailed over a threshold. Though he did not know it, an imaginary line dividing the planet of his morality had been drawn over that patch of sea. A cloud passed over the face of the sun so the deck was suddenly cast in shadow and in that moment Cowell slipped into the darkness of his captain's mind. He became an intruder moving through a house and trying its doors. Not tampering with anything but thinking of shifting its furniture. The *Waterloo* slid into the distance. I strained and heard Stewart's thick rambling voice, '. . . that bastard Guard will be damned before he fills his boat with my native flax . . .'

Cowell turned and walked away, disappearing beneath the deck, and Clementson watched him go. At that moment Clementson looked like a man who had felt the wind change but could not tell the precise angle of the new breeze. A fear, very faint, very lonely, was written on his face, as though in his bones he had felt a slight but sudden drop of pressure in the middle of a sunny day, forecasting a storm, or sensing one miles away. In his sailor's superstitious science a small breeze was always the edge of a storm. A cool gust suddenly creeping over the skin of an arm that had been warm in the sunlight meant a dragon, thousands of leagues north, raging over the heart of the Pacific, black clouds its thunderous belly, green waves rising like monsters' wings. When he saw me looking at him he quickly turned around to face the sea ahead of us. Shoulder to shoulder with his captain at the prow, their backs to us as we sped into the south.

That evening I stood next to Cowell in the fading light, above the deck, in the dark rising. I strived to measure the ease of manner between us. I strained to feel a change in his bearing, to sense the barest magnet's quiver, but there was none. If something had shifted inside him by a few degrees during the minutes of that afternoon when the sky had suddenly darkened into an omen, he had carefully reassembled the machinery of his calm face so everything was once again received and dispersed as knowledge. He smiled as he spoke, with the assurance of a sextant, his young eyes moving upon an ageless sea. But I watched his smile carefully. For that afternoon I had felt the sea change when Cowell had gone below deck, as though he had abandoned us or something of himself, his theories of distance or trade or translation. The world had shifted beneath us: I had seen it and I knew what I had seen. A pact had been made before me. Someone's fate had been sealed. And yet Cowell was easy and relaxed as we spoke in the clear cool evening on the deck of our ship. Such was his calm that I soon forgot to watch him. There was no searching the evidence of his manner, its gentle rise and fall.

Instead I could feel his stories beginning. I detected the thinness that hovered in the way all his stories started. A gentle net was cast out in his concentration, gathered back to himself and slowly emptied of its contents which he spread on the ground before him. He eyed and spoke the jewels and rocks he found. He laid them in patterns and picked up his thread of story from the space between them.

'So. The thirtieth of September,' he said.

'And tomorrow October,' I replied.

'Tomorrow an island fortress will appear before our bow. An island small and steep and black, a spiked Saxon shield afloat in the sea. Entry Island, called Kopitee. Tomorrow we sail into the heart of the Wolf, a dark heart which knows only its own language.'

Night fell and we moved off to his cabin.

The first time the Great Wolf saw Kopitee it was an island already occupied, shared by the people of three tribes. Te Rop'raha, travelling south in a war-party, saw it from the cliffs atop a western shore and under his breath he swore to take it. It was a quiet afternoon. The clouds were calm over the water where the black island sat, whale-back in the sea. The peaceful men of that island were not to know that the Wolf had looked upon them, that the overtures of war had been made. But to the old chief, Tufaray, who stood with the Wolf that day, Te Rop'raha said, 'I will tear them asunder.' Tufaray looked across the water and saw the red slaughter waiting to happen.

Tufaray had been a young man, a strong new king, when the first English ships broke the horizons of the clear, green world all around him. Those strange ships sailed at the watery edge of the blue planet, against the far rim of existence. Men with brown faces watched the sea from their low hills and beaches. Goblins sailed those ships, men said. The white-skinned spirits of the sea were sung beside fires, chanted and woven into new histories, and over the years, while he grew into an old man, Tufaray watched those ships and learned their ways. Strange flocks of sails moving upon the waves.

In this way old Tufaray had become a reader of seas and skies. That calm afternoon when he stood shoulder to shoulder with the Great Wolf, their hearts joined in the forge of plunder, he spied the broken rig of a northern ship far below them, its wood-wrecked ribs and sail-torn carcass strewn upon the beach, a giant dead octopus. When he saw it wrecked there he read months of sea-traffic ahead. He knew the goblin-sailors would bring guns and powder to those beaches.

To the Wolf Tufaray said, 'These spirits have hearts made of trade and iron. For pigs' meat and potatoes they'll pay tobacco, rum and blankets. For flax they'll pay muskets. Trade with them and you'll become a great chief, wearing slaves in a necklace round your thick young neck. Go home to the north and return with a force. Tear open the ribs of these hills and cup the heart of commerce chambered in this chest. Make ready for the conquest of this country.'

And the Wolf replied, 'Then I will take this island, Kopitee, and forge from its fens a fearsome fort, a spiked nest of war, an isle-den, sea-surrounded, that none will take from me. My island will be the shield and the spear, the cloak of comfort and the claw of fear of all men.'

So Te Rop'raha returned to his home in the north, a migratory bird on a wandering wing, home to nest in the mire, guided by instinct and a buried desire. He sat quietly upon the land and sang no word or prayer for the warm winds of war that he waited for through cold winter days. Neither fence of spear nor wall of fire did he raise. Frozen rains and smoke lay thick on his wooded coastal country. All about him the ditches and banks were empty of birds' nesting. And he sat quietly upon the earth waiting for the season of war.

V.

Migration of Fire

We carried 200 barrels of fresh water from Australia.
When these were emptied we refilled them from streams in
New Zealand.

Other liquids we carried:

30 gallons of vinegar.

5 bottles of pepper sauce. We wished we had more.

2 dozen cans – weighing 2 lb each – containing soup made
from leeks and potatoes. We soon wished we had some
other variety. Oh for a pumpkin. A tomato.

2 bottles of lime syrup.

20 puncheons of rum, for trade, and 5 more puncheons for
our own use.

We knew of 2 further gallons stored in the ship's medical
cabinet, kept for emergencies. (There were several
emergencies, always late at night or in the early hours of
the morning, and always in Cowell's cabin.)

We carried half a gallon of port wine, also for medical
purposes.

Half a gallon of brandy, likewise.

Blend whisky (a two gallon cask) which bore an unhappy
resemblance to the ship's store of turpentine (half a
gallon) and copal varnish (4 gallons).

24 gallons of linseed oil.

Half a gallon of Japanese varnish.

4 gallons of whale-oil for burning, and for lighting our
cabins.

A small measure of iodine and other small measures of
liquid medicines in the medicine chest.

Various paints: pounds of ochre, lampblack, Prussian blue,
chrome yellow. White lead, chrome green, red lead,
verdigris. Burnt umber.

Coal tar.

Our ship sailed with tons of barrelled liquids inside her.
Wooden hearts. Our ship sailed and rolled on the sea like
a giant cask.

We kept space aside for flax. We had room enough for
some seventy tons, or so Cowell reckoned. We carried most
provisions in barrels. We had a cooper's department on
board, Swann had a carpenter's shop.

We carried empty barrels (1000 spare oil-casks) but could
have made more.

2 ½ tons of hoop iron.

8 pine and spruce planks, of assorted lengths.

200 feet of white pine lumber.

350 feet of cedar boat boards.

40 feet of oak plank.

24 boat timbers.

12 boat knees.

2 boat stems.

A boat keel.

A spare royal.

A spare topsail.

A spare mainsail.

A spare topgallant sail.

Spares of each of the above sails for the foremast.

A spare trysail.

A spare boommainsail.

Two extra studding sails.

A spare fore staysail, jib, and flying jib.

We carried so much wood and so many spare sails it felt as though we carried another whole boat inside us. The parts of another *Elizabeth*, a ghost *Elizabeth*, who could have been born at sea.

And we could have made her for we carried the tools.

We carried an anvil.

4 cast-steel hammers, as well as dozens of other hammers of other varieties.

4 vices. (Not counting our love of drink, our desire to fornicate.)

Various planes (smooth, hollow, and round).

Various gimlets, punches, files, chisels (socket and scarfing).

100 lb rivets, various sizes.

A grindstone.

2 whetstones.

Various saws (hand, compass, and splitting).

3 crosscut saws for timber felling.

Various hatchets.

Knives.

Several axes. Dozens of axes and flints for trade.

Hundreds of pounds of scrap lead, sheets of metal.

Hundreds of pounds of nails, a wooden box of old bolts.

Dozens of other tools, but among Swann's most treasured
    possessions were:

A carpenter's rule, and

A carpenter's horse.

The carpenter's rule, Swann explained to us a thousand
times, was never ride a carpenter's horse. His humour
was a sad thing. He was better at repairing holes in walls
or nailing down lifted floors. Or talking about native
trees. Swann spoke favourably of New Zealand woods: a
pleasing hardness to work with, desirable when making
spare spars. He predicted a timber trade one day in this
country. Even during the days on which he had no work he
could be found in his small carpenter's shop working with
a length of native timber. He had procured it during our
first days in New Zealand waters, when we lay in harbour
far to the north, where we saw the straightest and tallest
trees growing handy to the shore. And green! Such a
brilliant green – not the black-green of the deeper, valley-
hidden, and more treacherous trees in the forests I had
taken to wandering through, but a green made of honey

and sunlight. These enormous coniferous timbers. Such straight grains.

Swann had taken a length from a younger, slimmer one that grew among those giants. In the *Elizabeth* it stood angled against the natural slant of the ship's inner wall, held in a cross-bracing of planks of Swann's making. Wooden shackles. Throughout the voyage we were making down the island's side, down towards Entry, it had stood like a native prisoner in irons below deck. Unspeaking, unsmiling, without language or gesture. A strange, rough surface, but beautiful. Over the days, as we sailed south, Swann, below deck, chipped at its highest outer layers and slowly exposed the perfect smooth flesh of timber beneath the crusted cloth of bark. He found and unlocked a voice within its pure, even grains, an evenness of form, an order within it that could be listened to and made gentle. A shape emerged as though from a chrysalis, for Swann carved only the timber's upper reaches, bringing only those depths of wood to daylight, exposing only those to the air, to the space of human touch. Those curves of shoulder.

Eventually we realised it was the shape of a woman he was carving. Below her pleasantly full-bellied torso the bark of the timber remained untouched, so it seemed to me she wore something like the grass-skirts of the natives. Swann called her his New Zealand girl. Behind her back he carved her hands. A flowing mane of hair, a rippled wave. Each day the girl became clearer. Her breasts more shapely, her collarbone deeper. Her cheeks finer, her eyes rounder. We could feel she was good luck.

What would we call her? we wondered between ourselves.

'Elizabeth? After the boat?' suggested Swann.

'Mary. After the holy mother,' suggested Richardson, a man of equal parts superstition and faith.

'Constance. After my mother,' said George Brown.

'I would like to meet your mother,' said the Watcher, his rough hand cupping a full wooden breast.

But in the end she was never named. We called her the girl below deck and more rumours followed. Swiftly and easily corrected. Swann intended her as a decoration for the prow, a good spirit pointing our way. The men found her a source of encouragement. A ship needed a figurehead.

But Swann's carved lady never made it above deck. She was never affixed beneath our bowsprit and she never led us into a friendly port laden with traded riches. She stayed a prisoner, half-born in the stomach of the boat. I heard, months and years later, Swann still crossed himself whenever our voyage in the *Elizabeth* was mentioned, whenever he heard our ship's infamous name. I heard he blamed himself for everything that happened. For it was bad luck to carry a woman on board. And though Swann had meant his carved lady to be a charm for safe breeze, a calm in angry seas, he had left her incomplete. Half-carved, she lay below deck, inverting the power of heaven she had been meant to embody.

So the *Elizabeth* sailed to Entry with no carved lady to lead her. We spied that island on the morning of the first of October. It was a Friday. When we saw it we knew that it had been waiting for us. We knew in our bones that it had seen us coming.

We'd weighed anchor early that morning. At that hour the New Zealand sky was clearer than the clearest English day. A blue, blue sky rose over a blue, blue sea. We sailed south-south-west to find the fullest breeze, away from the coast we'd been following. As we moved further from the country its green sides darkened into black then faded out to a purple kind of blue.

We ate our breakfast – the best of the week, for it was always larger and more leisurely on a Friday – and we watched the land becoming more distant behind us. We drank tea from tin mugs and saw New Zealand lying like an animal in the ocean, the back of a sea-creature rising, a tail and a fin stretching far to the north behind us. And then someone called 'Land!' from towards the front of the ship. We turned and saw, far distant in the south-west ahead to starboard, the clear blue ranges of mountains floating on the sea. With land both before and behind we felt as though we were entering a wide bay whose jaws had opened around our brig. In front and either side of us lay land, miles and miles off. But Clementson pointed ahead of us to starboard and said, 'Those are the northern sounds of the Middle Island. We have no business on that island.' And he gave instructions to turn the brig back towards the coast of the Northern Island which we'd sailed away from that morning, for off that coast lay Entry.

So we bore east-south-east and the land rose slowly larger before us again, becoming clearer and blacker and greener as we trod the water towards it. But as we sailed nearer, the coast moved and changed shape before our eyes; we noticed a darker shard, a black headland emerging from its wooded side. And then this piece of land broke away completely from the Northern Island. We realised it was a black elbow afloat in the wide gulf of the ocean. A small island like a war canoe.

We saw its dark green folds and as we approached we could pick a steep-faced flank making a sheer side of its western edge, a shard in the water.

And in that moment a dream from days before came back to me and out loud I said I had dreamed of this island. The others to whom I had told my dream raised their doubting eyebrows, for the island in my dream had been covered in snow and ice and the very sea had leaped at it as if the world had been torn asunder in an earthquake sent from the mouth of God, but I said again I had dreamed of this island.

We all knew what island it was. We'd all imagined this spiked fortress of war, this war-fast isle, this deadly animal. It lay there calm and small and quietly, anciently, beautiful. It lay in wait there. We felt it watching us.

'Entry,' said Stewart.

'Kopitee,' said Cowell.

It was the first of October. It was a Friday.

In the afternoon we sailed around Entry, carefully keeping our distance. It lay like a Wolf, guarding the edge of the Northern Island. We approached as though we were wary of surprising it and as we approached we saw that it was larger than we'd thought. We felt its weight as though it was a planet. We could feel its gravity as we entered its waters and as we entered its orbit we became a moon to it. But we were only one of its satellites. Though we'd beaten Guard on the run we'd made to Kopitee, when we rounded the island's northern side we saw another vessel had already moored off its eastern coast. Someone recognised the *Dragon* of Hobart Town captained by a trader named Briggs. Clementson swore and Stewart kicked over a bucket of water. Kirkpatrick came forward and cleaned it up, for spilling buckets on board was bad luck. Stewart kicked Kirkpatrick up his young arse. Cowell said nothing. We sailed towards the coast of the Northern Island and found a place there to moor.

That afternoon men came and went from the shore but I passed those hours with Cowell alone in his cabin. The sun slid down the round, blue wall of sky, a yellow splash on the frame of porthole and the afternoon wore on. I drank tea from a tin mug. I smoked my pipe. And out there I saw Kopitee and thought of the Great Wolf talking to the trader called Briggs. We'd arrived suddenly into his world. He was there in the cabin, a shadow in the room, held in Cowell's voice, the young warrior chief standing where we'd left him, balanced on the thin edge of a war.

Let me tell you the story of the burning house.

Te Rop'raha wandered through a long winter, drifted through its smoky dusk evenings, a shadow walking between the thicknesses of trees. He roamed the country

103

about his home, a protective spirit about his village standing on its hill beside the sea. Musk of winter wood, unwoven smoke, he wore, seeped into his feathered cloak, into his hair. He spoke to no man and men said he spoke only with the deities of the evening air. In the late afternoons he stood upon high ridges and men saw his shape make a black silhouette against the frozen orange sky. Men said he could read the deaths that were written there.

Out of the north came the news a woman had died, a cousin to the youngest wife of Te Rop'raha. The Wolf went to this young wife, sixteen years old, and lay with her. Afterwards, while she was still wild with mourning, he released her into the north, to the funeral, all alone. Through broken country she walked in the high wind and rain till she came to the provinces of a fierce clutch of powerful tribes. These were the Wy-ka-taw, who lay along the Wolf's northern border, who were constant teeth in the wind against the forests of his northern forearm. Their name was taken from the great river: wide giver of water, green aorta of the Northern Island. Across vast fertile districts they lay like an outspread hand, a tangled net of alliances and marriages. The wife of the Wolf drifted through this landscape, through these acres in their thousands tilled and tightly bound by the shifting allegiances made upon it, sent there in grief by her husband Te Rop'raha.

She was found by a war-party, delirious and hungry and alone, wandering like a lost lamb. They slit her throat and drank the blood from her severed head. They cut her body quickly into pieces and packed these into baskets which they carried away.

High in the trees above, the Wolf watched in silence while these men of an enemy tribe carved his slain wife into joints of meat, making a feast of the body he'd slept against three days before, of the woman whose grief he'd borne and handled delicately in his strong hands. Over the previous days and nights of her solitary wandering he'd guarded her and watched her, following her unseen, passing through the treetops like a native brown parrot, a phantom of the trees. And though he had accompanied her through those days of her grief, raining and alone, he had stayed carefully hidden from her. Not once had he gone to her, so when she'd walked into death she'd walked alone and yet not alone. Though he had travelled with her like a companion animal or a spirit guide, she'd felt his absence within her, sharply, like a lack of food.

After her body had been removed from the glade where she'd been slaughtered and quartered, the Wolf fell to the earth. He knelt there and gathered handfuls of soft soil from where the blood had been spilled. He tasted that soaked dirt and swallowed the warmth of his wife's body. He prayed for the departed soul. He wiped his face with those warm and bloody handfuls. Then he stood and returned into the south, taking with him news of the crime he had just witnessed, the blood of his dead wife still on his face, for there he wore just cause for war.

War came like a flood.
Relentless months

of blood
like rain.

――――――――――

The years of war passed. When Te Rop'raha's houses were
lost and his villages taken; when his warriors fell defending
the shores of his lakes and his wide harbours; when his
young kinsmen's heads were removed from their bodies
where they lay; when a native raven harvest lay whitening
on the plain; even then, in the fires of a falling war Te
Rop'raha's mind turned to his anchor upon the ocean, the
crown of island afloat in the clear, shining sea far to the
south, a black jewel whose price was his lost war.

Te Rop'raha and his people had been pushed to the end
of the world, pushed back to the very edge of the earth
and sea. Quietly they waited for the end to come to the last
village on a hillock above the sand. They stood, a doom
of fifteen hundred, with their backs to the sunset, their
last evening on earth lit with this presage of fire, their
tribe a wooden ship sinking as the sun fell into the sea.
In the nearby woods they heard the rabble's nearest edge
creeping closer. They heard the sounds of sticks being
broken in the forest. These, they knew, would be gathered
together and made into bundles, a hundred faggots set
alight and cast over the walls of their fortified village. In
the hours after night fell they would be flooded, overrun
by the rising tide of their enemies, a tribe submerged in
darkness and flame, their songs burnt down and leaving
no echo but the lapping of the waves on that quiet beach.

Still Te Rop'raha stood on the high wall overlooking the land outside, his arms folded before him in defiance, his cloaked back offered to his people like the inside of a chiefly shield, lined with rabbit's pelt and a handle of studded leather. There was the small sound of a child crying and the Wolf spoke without turning, 'Make quiet that child or I will make my breakfast from it.'

After the sun had fallen behind the edge of the sea, in the half shadow of twilight, Te Rop'raha led his people from their village to the quietness of the beach, its wide sandy margin, mauve in the darkening world around them. They looked out upon the ocean and saw a darkness of canoes, black hands reaching to them across the low waves under the indigo sky. They huddled on the beach and waited for the final onslaught from the sea. When the war-craft drew up on shore the warriors they contained stepped slowly onto the beach. There was no charge or battle-cry. Then Te Rop'raha's people looked and saw that the invaders carried neither spears nor axes but instead brought with them hot baskets of fish and steaming sacks of potatoes. This was an invasion of saviours. Their leader came to Te Rop'raha.

'So your canoes have saved me,' said the Wolf.

'Aye, cousin,' said the other, and then they bent their heads and pressed their noses together in the way of local greeting.

On the beach the two men walked in conversation while behind them the people of two tribes sat on the sand and ate together as the stars came out above their heads.

On these islands to send a storm of spears is to receive

a breeze of muskets. There are laws of the land that seem like laws of nature, like cycles of seasons with their irresistible rise and fall, in their swelling and easing, the way the stacking of hay can point to both the industry and the rhythm of the wet earth. War is another tide, another phase of moon. It turns and returns upon itself and afterwards peace, when it rises, rises less like smoke and more like the calm on a still harvest morning, a clear yellow sheen on the clear new wall of the day or the warm carried within a young summer. When Te Rop'raha's cousin landed on the beach with potatoes and fishes, he landed with a seasonal warmth carried onto the beach of a dying world. He brought the ritual of food, the rites of defeat, to a tribe that stood on the brink of extinction. On these islands wars can be ended in this way. Enemies could eat together, the vanquished fed by the victors, before the defeated ceded their tribal lands forever to their conquerors and were allowed to leave and make new homes. This was an ancient code of war, a rhythm of the familial earth upon these islands where chains of marriages and families made for alliances were draped between vast provinces. Friends and enemies formed galaxies of common cause across the entire country. The Wolf knew how these lines were drawn. He could recite them. He was fluent in the ways that the human element shaped every pattern made upon the earth. In such a way he grasped the mind of his cousin, a man who was now married into the alliance which had been forged to fall against him, but was bound too by the honour of blood to protect him. So although the Wolf was on one side and his cousin on another, when Te

Rop'raha made the fiercest of wars he knew that he fought an enemy whose own spears could be used as a shield against them.

'So your canoes have saved me,' said Te Rop'raha to his cousin as they walked on the beach.

'Aye, cousin. But not this harbour, not these sands,' replied the other.

'Not these sands,' repeated the Wolf, 'but sands far to the south. I will lead my people there.'

Then he called out to his people on the beach and he promised them an island. Though he had made them into refugees he promised them a migration of fire. They would be made into a canoe and they would sail south over the land. They would be borne on the breath of the god of war, carried south on that air till they struck a secure island, a rock jutting like an elbow from the ocean, an island surrounded by sea and forts, safer than any island fen-surrounded. He would carry them there, steering them in the canoe he had made of them.

Then he stalked back up the hillock of sand overlooking the beach and re-entered the gates of his last village. He heard the enemy still swarming in the forest beyond. And while he heard them snapping twigs in their hands and breaking branches across their knees as easily as if they were the dry and weakened bones of dead birds, he knelt before his chiefly house, the house of his fathers, and laid a nest of dried scrub and kindling there. Then he set his carved house on fire and watched the years burn. He stood, the black shape of a man spread like a stretched hand against the flames, and it seemed that he burned like an effigy, an ancestor of war, his spirit climbing into the coal sky along with the men whose bodies had been translated into carved thighs and shoulders by chisels years ago, now released by holy fire, turned into smoke to float free of the tribal anchors of land, to drift south on the evening wind in the shape of a Wolf on the air. Above the cracking of fire his voice rose in a lament. As his village was devoured in flame, as his chief's heart ascended in a bonfire, he chanted from the burning palace of the blood of years.

> *A farewell to land:*
> *Calm Water, your name is Hawneepaka.*
> *Alas, how we hold you far away.*
> *Alas, we depart from you*
> *forever.*

Our first evening at Entry. We lay in sight of her, moored off the Northern Island. Men came and went to its near shore through the afternoon. Cowell and I and a few others took a late skiff and joined the men already camped on the beach. There we watched the night fall through its sunset colours. Beyond Kopitee clouds a hundred miles long arced high above the earth, brilliant streaks of coloured ribbon. The sky felt like a festival and Kirkpatrick, lying near me, murmured something about a maypole. He spoke quietly, perhaps not wanting the others, the rougher men, to hear him, and yet I think he wanted strongly to say to someone what it was he saw in that strange sky made at the bottom of the world. I rested my hand on his knee.

We lit a small fire on the beach, a small shrub of orange flame planted where the golden green tussocks grew out of the sand. Behind us the land turned to thicker bush and scrub. Before us lay the wide beach and then the heaped and forested slopes on the back of Kopitee rising purple and grey and blue and black from the flat shining sea. There we lay smoking our pipes. Men spoke between themselves.

Cowell stretched and then stood and shook himself and as he re-lit his pipe he told us how the Wolf used fire as a signal to passing European ships, how a fire atop his island was an invitation to trade. We looked at Kopitee and saw the thick orange swirl of sun sinking into the highest point of the island's back. We saw her all aflame, made into a burning ember beneath a blazing sky, afloat in the sea. We sat there quietly, quietly struck by Cowell's way of arranging and imparting the world to us, his remarking upon trade fires timed to coincide with the precision of the sun, the whole earth turning on his voice. We sat there quietly while it slid, the sun, gradually, quickly, like thick liquid, from our view.

Stewart broke in on our thoughts: 'I see no fire!' he cried, shading his eyes and staring into the sunset. He cursed the harsh rays, trying to make out the beacon which he'd hoped to see lit upon the island, and I saw Cowell's eyes narrow and his head turn away. The captain was not one of us. Where the rest of us had seen the trick of a flame conjured by Cowell's words out of the very sun, Stewart had knelt and rubbed his eyes and sworn he was going blind in the damned savage light.

Some of the men grinned slyly among themselves. They were sailors most of them, men of the hardened sea, yet within them they carried moments which could be treasured unexplained, unspoken, until the time came for them to be uncovered and revealed to others, shared moments of holy sunlight in strange skies, a sunset dark and red and hung behind endless miles of the gilt-edged silver sea. The shadows of high mountains where no man had ever walked, or a bird no sailor could name circling us for half an hour in a deserted sea before disappearing into the frozen air of the south towards its undiscovered countries. The unknown world was so large around us. We carried its beauty inside our minds and our bodies and then passed it around between us in conversation in the same way that we passed around tobacco, tamping our pipes, heads down in concentration while Cowell spoke for us the country where we were moored, the doorstep we were stationed upon, the quiet beach.

We ate by the fire which grew brighter and richer, hotter as the night around us cooled. We turned the spigot of a cask of rum. We lay with our backs in the sand still warm from the fallen sun. Men told stories and my mind wandered up and down this beach, reached over the short miles to Kopitee. We drank and night fell deep and proper.

I thought about the young wife of the Wolf, released into the north in mourning, to the funeral of the dead cousin she would never reach. In my mind she would remain a woman wild in grief, nakedness breaking through her grass skirts and cloak of torn flax. I would see forever her creamy brown thighs cut with licks of

bramble, her smooth princess's feet cut upon rocks, her
cheeks stained with tears running down her body with the
wild rain caught and gathered by her tangled black hair.
In that rainy weather I imagined her cradling his absence,
the lack within her, the grief like the emptiness of hunger.
Did she long for his loathsome arms around her in those
cold evenings when she was all alone? What comfort
could she have taken to know he was there, companion
to her wandering? I could not reach my hand out to feel
the shape of her grief. I could not reach through such
strange loneliness to feel the soft flutter of her mourning
woman's heart. To think of the Wolf in the trees above
her, shadowing her for the last days of her life, watching
over her like a native bird, part-angel, part-carrion fowl,
I imagined the black eyes looking from out of his face, a
place where you'd expect to find and look into a human
soul. Why had he followed her unseen, letting her wander
alone? I could not reach inside his mind to know what
light was there, but I felt a glimmer in the dark, a cruel
will. Had he watched over her wide-tracked wanderings,
gently guiding his young lamb to the lap of his enemy,
only to let her fall there and witness her end? Is that how
he had watched in silence, in stillness, while her throat
was slit and her body cut into pieces? Below him the men,
unsuspecting, cut her arms like joints of lamb, removed
the guts and piled them for the flies and native ravens, the
scavenger hawks. They spilled her blood in their muddy
ground. They made a patch of holy earth for the Wolf to
gather just cause for war by the warm handful, cupped and
spread across his face with an open palm. I imagined the

Wolf silently watching those butchers while they worked. Bent over their cut of meat, above them his weight shifting upon his bough, the only sound the wind gently creaking the branches of great trees, their rustling sigh.

Gathered on the beach, beneath the last light of the sky we heard the sounds of strange birds. Their sounds were strange sounds. We heard one nearer to us rising softly, repeating at short intervals. Though we knew it to be a bird its sound came to us like a human voice; we listened to its round vowels and imagined we heard English in them.

Cowell told us that other traders and whalers to those islands had begun to call this little night owl the More-pork after the English words they thought they could hear it calling out in the dark. And soon the drunken men were singing out those words to each other around the fire in high-pitched voices: 'More-pork! More-pork!' When the men had stopped their game, we realised the bird could no longer be heard. I imagine it had flown off amid our noise. I was sad to think of it taking offence to our mimicry. I liked the idea of that little bird listening to us and talking back. We liked the name, Morepork, with its plump, round quality. We never found out what the New Zealanders called it.

Then someone said quietly in the dark, 'I can see a fire.' And though we sat before a fire whose embers had grown thick and dragon-bellied over the hours of the night, to a man we turned away from those flames and instead looked out there to Kopitee, out towards where that dark island lay afloat in the midnight waters. There we saw a line of distant fires, a burning chain along its beach across the water. We did not know what it meant. Stewart rose drunkenly and bellowed out something to the rest of us about trade and flax. He believed that he had been called by the Great Wolf of Entry to negotiate business, but Cowell said calmly that those fires were no invitation to trade. The captain would not listen. He stomped across the beach to the skiff, his curses ringing out behind him as he reached the boat pulled up onto the sand. We heard his heavy, awkward body fall into it and a few moments later came the broken rhythm of his fretful snores. We let him lie there, imagining him to lie crooked in the bottom of the boat.

'Tell us about fires.'
    I'll tell you about fires.

Te Rop'raha knows fire
like he knows how to throw
his voice against the side of a room
and make a shadow on the wall
of a small man standing
ten feet tall.

Let me tell you about fires.
    We sat in the flame-licked darkness and listened to a story about fires.

When Te Rop'raha moved his tribe south, travelling around a hidden coastal highway, he travelled with fire. As his people moved through tangled wet forests they hung fires like lanterns from the branches of trees and found their way through the darkness of a wooded coast. They lit fires to heat the cooking-stones which they buried in the earth when they made ovens from the pores of the land. They went from their burning lands in the north southwards through trees like smoke, bearing fires till they came to this cool dark island in the sunlight at the corner of a bright sea. In this train Te Rop'raha led the women and the children, the old and the injured, and those near ruin. They were the baggage of Te Rop'raha's lost war, a limping caravan. In the slow winding years and months there were deaths of exhaustion and exposure, of old age and disease, and of war wounds that would not heal. So they travelled too with funeral fires. They hung the bodies of those who died in the trees, leaving the bones to rattle in the rainy wind after their convoy had moved on. They left a trail of wet ashes behind them like tears, for leaving the bodies of their dead hanging in the weather was both a pain and a comfort to them. They left corpses like dead leaves and rotting branches hanging from the trees.

In the first months of their great migration they moved between villages friendly to them. They would camp outside one village for a month and at the end of those weeks move to another nearby in the space of a few days. They followed a string of settlements over flat land like a river winding away into the south. For the first months they moved gently but then the land reared up and opened

its mouth of wild dangerous country. From the gates of
the last safe village Te Rop'raha looked south into a wall
of black and grey rain falling into sheer green valleys.
He knew that was unsafe territory; although it was not
enemy land, it was land into which an enemy would follow,
tracking them with scouts, waiting for them to wander
into steep gorges and drown in the dangerous rivers, to fall
from the sheer faces of mountains whose stony sides could
not be passed. Death waited for them in that country's
valleyed teeth.

Te Rop'raha chose to leave the village in an early
morning downpour. He took two hundred warriors with
him into the south, beyond the veil of falling water, leaving
all others behind. He meant to find a way through that
country, to prise open its jaws and lay a stick there: two
hundred men holding the way ajar for the fragile bodies
of thirteen hundred weakened souls to pass through like
a whispering, a sigh, an intake of breath moving through
those hills.

They travelled south swiftly, Te Rop'raha's two hundred,
making for a river called Maw-koh.

In fourteen days they struck its silvery waters.

They crossed it at midnight, a herd of black shapes
melting out of the trees and moving towards the water, and
passing through the water, and emerging from the water.
When they crossed the river they passed into the country
of a friendly tribe and the darkness of the land that had
been a danger was translated into a cloak of protection.
They walked through a night of blue hills. They followed
the moon and stars above them, visible through the black

lattice of trees. Through the hours they walked and in the frozen light of morning they strode through tussocks, spirits of a grey dawn.

They reached a village and little warblers sang their arrival.

They were welcomed and fed there.

But while they rested over a span of days Te Rop'raha thought about the trail they had found, the road along which a cargo of bodies could be passed as if ferried upon a secret forest river. He woke early on the third morning and could not fall back into sleep so he rose and went from the village, walking over calm hillsides in the hour before dawn. Though the energy of the day had not risen, there was a warmth within it, a wandering spirit stalking the land, an omen blooming in the open air, breathable. A blue flower drifted on the wind and landed at his feet. He bent and picked it up and saw that it was no flower he knew. He looked up and read the absence of birds in the clear sky.

He thought of his tribe, split in two, resting in safety to the north and the south, but he did not trust the ark of space in between, its dangerous cliffs high and dark, its palace of rains, its ravines. In those places rocks slid and rivers rose, erasing tribes and hiding enemies. He did not trust that space of high earth.

He walked back to the village and entered the hut where he had passed the night. He lay with his back to the bare ground and held the strange blue flower in his hands resting on his chest, twirling the stem in his fingers. The blue flower moving like a moth. A twitch in his mind like an insect while he stared unblinking at the low ceiling above him. He thought over the trail they had found. Four hundred feet had trampled those grasses. Like the path of a previous flood or a swollen river they had made the shape of an empty rib, a furrow against the dark green earth behind them. They had not found a trail but left one, Te Rop'raha thought.

At sunrise he rose again from the ground where he lay and went to the meeting house where his men slept. He passed silently inside and saw that large mats had been hung across the high open doorway, blocking out all light so the men could rest in peace. He moved through the darkness through the sleeping two hundred, kneeling and gently patting their bodies, the shapes of the blankets they slept beneath. Whenever he found a musket he drew it slowly from the body it lay beside or beneath, undoing tight knots of fingers without breathing or blinking so the guns they clasped could be removed and carefully replaced with spears or with the handles of axes. He worked in this way for half an hour, a thief moving through sleeping graves, searching, stealing, and replacing. Those two hundred bodies yielded twenty-four firearms. He laid these upon the ground beside him at one end of the meeting house and then sat and waited for his men to wake. Whenever a young man stirred and woke the Wolf went to him, handed him a musket and told him to get up. In this way he found and armed his twenty-four fittest warriors. He led them from the shadows of the carved house into the sunlight, and from the calm sunlight of the village into the hills from which they'd arrived, back along the trail they'd found and made in the days before. In the days afterwards, to avoid being seen, they travelled only at night. During the day they rested and hid themselves in caves, wet clefts in the sheer thighs of the country. On that journey they lit no fires. They broke no branch and spoke no word over and above a whisper. They passed along the trail like they were hardly even there. They were less than ghosts, less even than the memory of ghosts.

In the north, encamped, sheltered and protected, the thirteen hundred waited for Te Rop'raha to return. Then, more than a month after he'd walked away into the south, he reappeared to them in the dawn of a clear morning, twenty-four armed warriors behind him. They moved into the temporary city of tents outside the walls of the village and Te Rop'raha called to his people to prepare for the hills. He walked down the makeshift avenues formed between one canvas shelter and the next and watched as his women and old men and children stowed their precious tools for cultivation, their sacred heirlooms. Small wind instruments of bone and green-stone combs. Flints for wood and food and fires. He saw the containers his people carried, the gourds of water and wooden treasure boxes, the baskets of pork and bags of potatoes. He saw the bundles of sacks they carried, the cloths and blankets, woven and made in Europe and brought here in the deep hulls of wooden ships and acquired in trade. He stopped when he came to a group of women, five wives to the same husband, packing their family's things. Each woman carried on her back a large roll of red cloth. He ordered them to take the cloths from their backs and tear them into strips.

When the tribe took its first slow steps into the south,

each man, woman and child walked wearing a piece
of red ribbon ripped into a sash or a crudely torn cape.
And as they moved slowly away, Te Rop'raha ordered the
twenty-four men bearing arms out into the wild country
all around them. He sent them in every direction. He told
them to spread the rumour of a war-party cutting a swathe
through the hills into the south, thirteen hundred strong
and clothed in red. For the Wolf knew that no passage of
guns was possible, only the myth of fire, wrapped about his
people like torn strips of red cloth. He told his twenty-four
to wait for the tribe at the river.

So Te Rop'raha led his refugees through the high and
dangerous country with only a rumour to protect them,
an illusion, a red fabrication. They made their way in a
slow caravan of blood, a single line, an artery a mile long
winding through the mountain rainforest.

The Wolf paused in the slow, steady stream of his
people whenever the wind changed or the sky darkened
overhead. He stopped to consider the angle of a stone or
the configuration of wet pebbles by a stream, the freshness
of the arrangement as though it was the shit of a wild
animal. He searched a hundred familiar scents for the one
that was unfamiliar, the smell of the footprint he didn't
recognise. He looked for the shaking tree in the place
where no tree should have been shaking. He read the sky.
Occasionally when he passed a black stump standing and
rotting in the wet earth he cast a small swatch of red cloth
upon it, frayed and hanging as though caught by accident,
torn from the hurrying body of a passer-by. From time to
time having crossed a small stream he cast a handful of

gunpowder into the soil of the bank and laid a footprint clearly upon it. He left behind him deliberate traces, small odours of his giant red animal of war.

Somewhere across a wide gully a scout crept carefully, a boy in the undergrowth crawling away from the red shapes he saw moving through the trees half a mile to the south. His savage young heart beat quickly in his chest. He did not know if he'd been seen.

Each night when the sun began to leak from those forest gullies Te Rop'raha halted. During the last hour of available light the men and women and children set down their loads and scoured the hills for kindling and dry wood. Every evening they gathered enough fuel for five hundred fires to burn through the night until the first glimpse of dawn. During the hours of darkness, if an enemy spy looked down into the gully where the refugee tribe was camped, he would see the necklace of amber lights burning below, a glowing line a mile and a half long. From that height it seemed as though a crack had opened in the wooded rocky side of the earth to reveal the burning core of the world.

The boy followed the red tribe for days from a safe distance high above the gullies, walking under the ridges of sky unseen. One night he sat high on the shoulder of a valley looking down upon the beauty of their fires. For two weeks he'd followed this party, without daring to come too close, without knowing who they were. But that night he descended towards their flames through the thick cover of scrub, through the safety of wide black trees and heavy-leafed ferns. He crept lower towards them and stopped at a safe distance, not close enough to see their faces but close enough to hear their voices, close enough to hear a baby crying and the soft clucking of the woman soothing it. He crept closer, through his curiosity, until he saw. This was not a war-party but a migration. And so he knew then that he'd found the disappeared tribe of Te Rop'raha. He climbed quickly out of the quietly burning valley.

The tribe limped on through the days, their red ribbon winding through green rainforest. At night they rested beside their burning chain and in the mornings when they drifted they left a trail of ashes and blackened ground behind them, the wide, burned footprint of their slow flood towards the river Maw-koh.

As they moved along their trail Te Rop'raha took to walking a little way away from them, above their course, through the dense rainforest near the skyline. That was where the forest was thickest; that was where spies would follow. So Te Rop'raha walked there, stalking his own from the shadowy place of an enemy mind and as he walked he read every mark in the earth. When he found a nest of broken branches and a trail climbing the side of the hill he saw that someone had followed them for a time and then left the valley. He did not know if they had been abandoned or discovered. There were signs in nature that could be read but not easily understood. The sudden silence of animals in warm weather could signal the approach of either an earthquake or lightning; red light before the sun rose in the mornings could mean either high wind or hard rain. So those broken branches meant they had been seen, but they did not say by whom. Had it been a

solitary wanderer, far from home, who had shared part
of their course through the dangerous hills and followed
them and rested with them, whose loneliness of days had
driven him to seek the comfort of their fires at night? Or
had it been a scout who roved like the eye or moved like
the hand of a dangerous tribe reaching into dark places
to throttle the necks it found? Had it been a tracker from
a northern tribe who knew the scent of Te Rop'raha? Had
they been hunted?

The tribe wound their way through the days while Te
Rop'raha walked the skyline above, watching the hills
behind for any sign of a returning enemy, a troop raised by
their scout.

On the twenty-fourth evening of their high hill crossing,
Te Rop'raha, standing sentinel on a high ridge, heard the
echo of rushing water carried to him on the back of the
cold southerly breeze. It was the Maw-koh river, a mile
away. He knew his guns waited for him there. Tomorrow
he would lead his people across the river and they would
pass over into the protection of a friendly tribe. This would
be their last night in this dangerous country. He descended
into the gully, towards the sounds of his tribe gathering
wood for the night's bonfires. And then he heard another
sound on the evening air. Quiet words spoken barely above
whispers in the strange voices of men not of his tribe. Like
a sinister wind they rustled in the trees around him and Te
Rop'raha saw that on this, their last night in this wild and
dangerous country, they were to be ambushed, slaughtered
in sight of the safety that waited for them a mile away.
Quietly, calmly, the Wolf descended to his people and

walked among them. He ordered them to light a thousand fires. He ordered them to pile every bundle and belonging of every person as high as a man, to stack them around the flames and cover them in red cloth, to cover every small bush with whatever cloaks they could find. After he gave this instruction he disappeared.

Night fell and his tribe waited obediently beside the fires and the bundles they'd made, near the shrubs they'd dressed in red. Calmly they sat, unaware of the enemy above them waiting for the full darkness of night to fall.

An hour later Te Rop'raha's voice rang out along the valley. A scream and a volley of shots tore the dusk and along the red mile of refugee fires the Wolf ran, a demon of war, suddenly alive among his tribe again. He had returned to them and brought twenty-four muskets with him, twenty-four armed men who ran back and forth between the fires, firing their weapons into the air, answering Te Rop'raha with shots and screams whenever he called out to an imaginary legion of warriors gathered along the red mile. To the enemy waiting silently above it seemed that many hundreds of warriors waited there, ready to repel the battle they had meant to bring in secret. When they heard Te Rop'raha calling out to his warriors to fear no wave waiting to break upon them from the ridges above they peered down through the trees and saw a valley dressed in red, thousands of shapes of men beside a thousand fires. They'd come to ensnare the refugee Te Rop'raha but instead they'd found a cauldron of war coming to the boil. They heard its shots and shouting. They would not drop into the valley that night.

They turned and melted back into the highest trees and crept away, disappearing back into the safety of a night without fires.

An hour later, from the valley below, Te Rop'raha led his people. They gathered their bundles from the places beside the fires where they'd made the impression of armed men and moved off as though it was the dawn. They left their fires burning behind them. They came to the river and crossed the river and wearily they climbed the long far side of the valley while the night around them stretched on. They slipped away.

But in the small hours the fires they had left behind them burned on, slowly dying. In those empty glades their flames quietly fell into thick beds of embers without a soul around to see them. Imagine walking into those groves, in that dark, along that trail: a thousand fires for a mile and a half, the trees hung with red cloth. Imagine the ghosts you would feel there.

And somewhere along the skyline above that burning chain lies the dead body of a young boy, the tracker who'd found and led the small army to Te Rop'raha and his limping tribe disguised as a war-party. Now he lies in the undergrowth, his young body, only fourteen years old, slowly returning to the earth through the passage of worm and dirt and rain. His neck was broken, snapped as easily as a baby rabbit's is snapped, the smooth brown skin bruised by the purple impress of strong fingers and thumbs. The men he'd led to that valley of burning fire had held him down while their chief silently squeezed the life from him, a punishment for his false report. They left him there on that ridge lying in the open air above an unintended memorial, the silent valley where the traces of torn red cloth still hang from trees gently moving in the breeze.

When Cowell finished speaking we stared into the small nest of flames. In the dark space left by his voice we heard the sea. The waves on the beach were small and shallow, not a foot high, and yet we could hear the steady sound of surf like a little wall, a little roar. The power of the wild ocean was always there on those islands, even on still nights on their calmest beaches.

'The fires are out,' said the Watcher. We looked to the island and saw he was right. I saw then that several men had fallen asleep where they lay as they'd listened to Cowell's stories. Like driftwood they lay in the sand, their shapes curled and sleeping. I wondered how far they'd travelled with the Wolf before abandoning him for their own rest and sleep had taken them. Perhaps even now, in their dreams, they moved along a forest trail in high hills of wind and rain. Perhaps they carried muskets and moved in a train. Perhaps they were natives now, clothed in red, or perhaps they had their own ruddy white skins and wandered beaches.

Cowell said he would take the first watch so the rest of us took what coats and things we had and made our pillows. I had a blanket and although it was a mild night still I wrapped myself within it. I curled and rolled over and fell asleep to the sound of soft sparks from the fire over the constant surf of the sea.

The next morning was the morning that Kirkpatrick found the sign of strange shells, written mysteriously on the beach a little way from where we'd slept.

I had woken that morning to the light of the sun, warm and new upon my face, filling my eyes. I watched it rise over the low foothills, to the north in the east, over their pale, clear shapes, green and blue, several miles away. We lay at the edge of the tussocks, where the sand was finer than on the beach, heaped upon little hillocks that made natural shelters against any wind. I thought about rising and making a fire to boil the water for tea and listened to the morning birds. To the left of me as I lay, inland, I could hear the singing of the forest. The percussive clicks and throaty calls rising to strange strings of whistles I knew to be the calls of the fat black birds whose feathers glowed green and brown, and from whose necks sprouted white tufts, worn like the rankings of Saxon chieftains. Four notes haunting and repeating meant the small bright green honeyeater, while the more ornate melody of higher notes was made by the little grey warbler. I knew their sounds as I knew the colours on their feathered backs. And to the right of me I heard the birds of the sea. Those were not songbirds but birds that called and screeched and cried: gulls and oystercatchers and others on long legs as practical as fishermen and trawlers and men who worked on wharves. So I lay between those two families of sound, the forest singers to the left of me and the criers of the shore to the right. And then above me, directly over us, flew two native parrots, their wings and bellies catching the low light of the rising sun so their undersides were lit up as red as embers. I had seen some of these birds before, alighted on branches and rummaging the undergrowth, and I knew them to be mostly as green as moss and brown as wood. But in the morning air, when they flew with no need of such camouflage, they carried the sunlight with them, beneath their wings. Their cries cut the air like sabres, harsh and mocking as they flew from their forest, swiftly across our margin of beach and out over the sea to the forests of Kopitee. I wondered if they nested on both islands, on Entry and the mainland, coming and going between them. I wondered if there was a word for a bird that made its homes on separate islands.

Eventually I rose and stirred the fire back to life from the previous night's embers. When the wood sparked and smoked thick and white, the men woke. While they waited for tea and breakfast some wandered the beach. Some reached for morning tobacco straight away and sat quietly smoking watching the fire or the sea. Some men were not talkers in the mornings, while others were boisterous, play-fighting like kittens or pups.

As our camp slowly stirred a thought struck me. When I woke there had been no one else awake. Cowell had taken the first watch but who had taken the second, the third, the fourth? Somewhere in the night our chain had been broken and we'd slept unguarded on that calm beach. I looked around me and saw that no one was missing. There was no unease amongst the men and I realised that as they had woken, one by one, they would have assumed that I'd been the last man on watch. I said nothing but thought on it. Perhaps Cowell, knowing something of these beaches and the Wolf on whose doorstep we lay, had decided a watch was unnecessary. I trusted his judgement but it disturbed me, if that had been the way of his thinking. I continued to stoke the fire and said nothing as I waited for the water to boil. Stewart was the last man to wake. We heard him rolling and moaning in the boat that lay twenty yards away, down near the sea. He groaned and emerged swearing bitterly about the crick in his neck. We had no sympathy. We thought him a fool. In that mood he would have punished any man for any reason. I decided then I would say nothing about the broken watch the night before. I let the matter go.

After breakfast I wandered the beach. Even at high tide its sands were wide and flat between the tussocks and the sea. Walking to the water from the fringe of grasses where we'd slept the sand was fine and light and soft beneath our feet. Closer to the water a straggled band of rotting logs and driftwood, black weed and grey stones marked the point of highest tide. This dark belt stretched the length of the beach as far as my sight could carry. Kirkpatrick and I walked between it and the water where the sand was damper, packed down smooth and dark and wet so our footprints stayed in the beach behind us. We walked in a southerly direction, the sun rising up the wall of blue sky behind and to the left, casting shadows on the sand in front of us to the right; we were sundials pointing to Kopitee as we wandered our way beside it.

It was an island with a live soul. Even without the Wolf who sat upon it and was embodied by it, dark and dangerous, calm and ancient and watchful in the water, that island had the spirit of a great creature of the sea. As I walked beside it that morning with Kirkpatrick I understood how the New Zealanders could tell the stories that they'd told Cowell, stories of an enormous fish that had been fished up from the deepest depths of the ocean and become the island whose back we walked upon. They had a presence, those islands, unlike any other islands I knew. I expected to see Kopitee open its fearsome eyes and look upon me as I gazed at it. I felt the sleeping intelligence of a large animal lying there and I wished to leave it undisturbed. Its dark green sides were so clear in the sharp light of the morning that I felt as though I could have reached over the five calm miles of water and touched it. I could have put my hands into its cage and stroked its wild flanks. Off its shore we could see that Briggs was still lying at anchor in one of the small northern coves. I saw his little ship there and imagined the island could have swallowed him whole.

While I thought these things Kirkpatrick walked ahead of me. I walked with my thoughts while he walked in wide circles, sometimes stopping and pausing to pick up shells or sticks or stones, the bones of fish. I watched him examine the wide swathes of black sand that had washed up onto the beach and left trails like dark branches making fingers against the sky. He turned to me and declared that it wasn't sand but wood, pulverised into small grains. He reckoned that a river must have carried rotting logs out to sea where they'd drifted on currents before being broken up and their remains deposited back on the shore. I half listened to him when he spoke to me. He had the manner of an engaged boy, explaining the world around him as far as he knew. I wasn't required to say anything in return. When he wasn't talking to me he walked ahead like a dog off the leash. At one point he stopped twenty yards ahead of me and turned to see where I was. There was something there he wanted me to see. As I approached he bent to the ground and plucked a shell from the sand. He held it out to me when I reached him.

'These weren't here last night,' he told me. I took the shell from him. It was largish and flat and white. I studied it for a moment then noticed Kirkpatrick's attention was not on the shell in my hands but on the sand around us, dark and shining and flat where it had been washed by the sea, free of the flotsam and jetsam of the shore. It lay like a dark piece of canvas, its perfect sand making a grain, a weave. And upon it, in a circle thirty feet across, I saw hundreds of shells laid upon the sand, arranged in two rows and making a spiral.

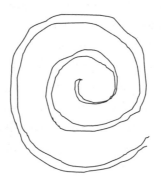

'These weren't here last night,' Kirkpatrick said again. He told me that he'd walked up and down the beach before the sun had set the night before. He said he would've remembered seeing such a strange and deliberate pattern. He stood there shaking his head while I said nothing. He asked me who could have put it there but still I said nothing.

We returned to where we'd made our camp and Kirkpatrick reported the curious sign we'd found further down the beach. Only a few men were there, the others having mostly returned to the ship or else, like Kirkpatrick and me, taken to exploring the beach. We led them back to the pattern, half a dozen curious men, Cowell among them. I stood near and eyed him carefully as he came upon those shells written in the sand like a letter from an unknown alphabet. I watched him for any glimmer of knowing, for the thought had occurred to me that Cowell himself had laid them there in the middle of the night. So for the second time in only a few days I found myself watching him closely, trying to detect the traces of any secret knowledge carried hidden inside him, a sign of his dark purpose. A few days before, when I'd strained to measure the sudden swerve in his way of being among us, when I thought he'd sworn a private oath against the ship and its captain, I had found no change in him. He'd stayed a ship's man. That morning as we looked upon that pattern, white and alien on the sand, I was relieved to see that his face was as blank and confused as any of ours. I was sure he knew nothing of those shells' mysterious authorship. He had no answer or explanation.

He was still with us, it seemed. Whoever had made that artistry of shells upon the beach, it had not been Cowell. But we listened to him describe what we saw in the sand about us.

He told us that the spiral was the form of choice among the native artisans. He told us that all knowledge could be contained within and carried by a spiral. He didn't tell us what that meant.

So it stayed on the beach as a signal we knew nothing about, a sign of arcane knowledge. We did not know who it was from or who it was for. We did not know if it was a welcome or a warning. We understood nothing of it, and yet we could not resist the temptation that it meant something. And if it meant something then we wanted to be able to read it, to translate it from its own dark time, from whichever dark mind had made it, and deliver it whole into a world of light. Above all we hated leaving the things we found unknowable. But we could not understand it and so eventually we found ourselves taking away its shells as mementoes. We drilled holes in them and wore them around our necks. We used the larger ones as plates and the smaller ones as cutlery, crude spoons for scooping beans. By midday the pattern we'd feared in the morning when we'd discovered it had been mostly removed from the face of the beach. Where it remained it lay like a depleted skeleton, an echo of itself, its mystery and strangeness reduced and its meaning shifted and removed. Its shells had been turned from the harbingers of a dark will into mere tokens, harmless shells which we translated into trinkets we could use and understand. So the New

Zealanders had left their footprint in the sand and we, when we found it, had re-shaped it to become more like one of our own.

Our first full day at Entry, our first day within its watchful distance, was the hottest day we'd had. It was a heat that fell upon us like a storm. We'd known cold and rain and spring breezes and now the heat of those islands bloomed like a bright flower filling our heads, enclosing us in its fist yet taking no energy from us. We could still move within our own skins. This was unlike the heat we'd known before when we'd sailed through the middle of the earth, around the seam of the spinning globe where the African heat had brought sickness, where heat rose in the mornings like a thunderclap and humidity fell over us like a blanket. We'd crossed the Indian Ocean, warmest of oceans, to Australia, the baked crust of a primitive earth that held a spirit of savage heat even in winter. The heat of these islands was sharp, like its light, but it was a joyful heat, a young heat from a playful sun crossing the sky. It scooped sea breezes from the surface of shining blue water and cast them over us. It was a heat that made deep wells of shade beneath the twisted trees whose black trunks rose into dark green and black leaves shining against that bluest of skies. Men took their shirts off and wound them into turbans. Our heads became shells, spirals of white linen. Our flesh was bitten and licked by the native sun, our white salty skins kissed and turned pink, cured into leather.

We passed the day.

Men sat together or else continued to wander the beach

or lay alone sleeping in the shade of trees further from the beach.

Kirkpatrick stood half a dozen sticks upright in the sand and retreated twenty yards to throw them down with stones.

Swann made a necklace of shells. Jewellery for his lady, he told us, but we did not know if he meant his half-carved darling below the decks of the *Elizabeth* or a sweetheart over the waves at home.

Shepherd made a sand castle.

We were waiting but we did not know what we were waiting for. We'd had no word from our captain or the mate. Both were upon the brig, Clementson having passed the night there and Stewart having taken the skiff back with a handful of men shortly after he'd woken. Whenever we looked to Kopitee we saw the *Dragon* still at anchor with her sails up. And *Elizabeth* stayed moored off our shore with barely a skeleton crew upon her. We did not know why Stewart waited. Cowell shrugged and said the captain would be watching the island. If the day seemed to pass peacefully between Te Rop'raha and Briggs, Stewart would approach Kopitee tomorrow.

In the afternoon eight men returned from the *Elizabeth* in the skiff with a load of empty barrels. We refilled them with fresh cool water from a stream a few hundred yards north of where we'd slept in the tussocks growing from the soft sand. The skiff went to and fro till late afternoon with loads of barrels, arriving on the beach empty and returning to the brig filled. The last time the skiff came to the shore our shipmates brought a few wrapped parcels of food. Biscuits, dried meats, a tin of tea, another of coffee. A few men went back to the ship but many of us chose to stay for our second night on the shore.

In only a day we'd become used to the lie of the land, the views that surrounded us there. We'd found a way of inhabiting the beach, or it had begun to inhabit us. We had nestled into our uneasiness, furnishing the strangeness at the end of the world with the routine that came when a day was spent in the one place. There was the stream we drank from, a couple of hundred yards north along the beach. Behind us, disappearing into the trees, the rumour of a path along which we knew we would find good firewood. Beyond that the green forested hills, so clear we could touch them though we reckoned them a day's walk there and back. When we closed our eyes we saw the shades of clear blue air; we saw green Kopitee behind. We saw the beach shining like dark glass when the water was at low tide. Fifty yards of hard wet sand left like a mirror by the sea's flat retreat, an oystercatcher standing there balanced upon its own perfect reflection. Our thoughts were clear and calm as we lay there and watched the day falling away. And in the south-west beyond Kopitee we could see the northern sounds of the Middle Island, forty miles away we guessed, though its shapes in the apricot sky were as clear as cut paper.

After the sun had set we saw a single star hung over those far silhouettes of hills. It shone as faint as the echo of a sleigh bell, a tiny white point nailed in the orange wall of sky. But as the sunset deepened and slipped darker the star shone brighter till we breathed the word

'Bethlehem' to each other. And though we knew it to be
Venus, when we saw it there brighter than we had ever
seen it before it could have been another star, a native
god, as if that country could have had its own planets
and heavenly bodies circling the skies above it. We asked
Cowell for its native name, for we felt that it ought to have
its own sound in those islands; there ought to have been
a local interpretation of its light. But Cowell said that if
there was a native name for that star he did not know it.
So we were left to wonder between ourselves if the New
Zealand name would translate more closely to Venus, or
Lucifer, or to another, altogether more tutelary god: one
that was neither a pagan goddess of love nor the spirit of
evil which men imagined to stalk the world but a calmer,
more distant power we would not understand. See the
way it hangs, Cowell observed, over the Middle Island, a
beacon for the Wolf whose mind and heart is bent on the
conquest of the southern island. I wonder, said Cowell, if
it hangs for him like a promise and a talisman. Remember,
he said, that there are histories as complete as tapestries
where doom has been written in the skies. Remember that
before the Saxon king fell upon his hill with a Norman
arrow slanting through his eye, it was a comet that
foretold the defeat of his army and the end of English
kings. Remember how we have a story of wise men
following a star beneath which was witnessed the birth of
Christ. It is in the nature of the sky to make signs for those
looking for them. Te Rop'raha has always moved south,
towards this star and towards the island rich with green-
stone beneath it. So perhaps for the Wolf looking south in

the evenings, Venus is a green-stone star, a star of War.

Those islands were islands of light though their heart
was dark to us.

We lit the fire while it was still light. We shared out
biscuits and pork and mutton for dinner and then, after
we'd eaten, Brown produced a sack and emptied an
avalanche of shells into a pot of water. Cockles. He'd
gathered them from the beach in the afternoon and now
sat cleaning them beside the fire while we looked on, our
interest undisclosed but undisguised. He'd brought garlic
from the ship, some butter and a little flask of wine. He
cooked them in a pan over the flames while each man sat
in silence and trusted the man next to him to say nothing
of this to anyone beyond the little circle gathered at that
occasion. Butter and wine were the ship's gold and suppers
of that sort were a serious and secret business. We ate
cockles in garlic and wine, with the taste of a strange sea
an echo in our mouths, a garnish.

'You get used to it,' declared Brown, breaking the silence
of the treasured meal. Men slowed their chewing, stopped
licking their oily fingers, and looked at him as though he'd
mistakenly revealed the previously unseen edge of a secret
society of men who ate special suppers away from the rest
of us. 'The strangeness, I mean,' he explained vaguely. 'The
being away constantly. You realise there is no idea of home
possible unless you are away from it. You learn the idea
that home is only an idea. Home and everything that goes
with it.'

As the men chewed their slow mouthfuls they dwelt
on Brown's words, measuring the truth in them against

whatever private knowledge they'd carried to this point, or whatever history had led them to be sitting here on this beach in the far south of the world, far away from the towns where they'd been born. Slowly, like the stars coming out one by one above, they said yes, they thought they knew what he meant. Some had been away from their homes five years, some four. Some three years, or two, or one. Some only the seven months since we'd sailed from England. Yet we were, all of us, constant travellers. That was our breed. We were closer – closer than we would ever guess – to that race whose paths we followed, Te Rop'raha's savage New Zealanders, who'd been travellers too down the same side of the same island we'd traced and made part of the countable earth. We shared a sphere, us and them. We were, both of us, parts of the continuous edge, round in all directions, wrapping the world. We were, both of us, hands passing over countries carrying an idea of countries. In our wooden hand, in our little ship which rounded the precarious corners of oceans, we'd brought things with us, intimate things we treasured, travelling symbols of all we'd left behind. Brown carried a certain spoon with him which, he said, came from the scullery in Saint James's Palace. At mealtimes he would take it from the chain around his neck and use it to eat native mashed potatoes or cress, or soups when he'd made soups. He was a tall lanky man. He didn't look like a ship's cook. When he ate on the shore he had a way of stretching back and lying on his side, propping himself up on his right elbow and looking out to sea with his calm clear eyes, savouring the traces of taste on the spoon he held in his mouth. I wondered if he imagined, behind his faraway eyes, the flavour of puddings made of custard and pears meant for princes when he tasted native potatoes, the smoky flavour of the earth of those islands.

As we travelled islands and beaches, passing through the stations of our journey, the things we carried took on new characters, new hints and tones. After months of drying my clothes upon a line hung across the deck of the brig I could see where the native sun had bleached the dark grey linen of my shirts. I liked to compare the lightened colour there with the material beneath the folds of collars, or inside the rough cuffs of my long sleeves, where the original dark hue of the cloth had remained. I liked having this record of the colour of the sun, for it reminded me of the warmth of its hand upon me. I wondered if, when we returned into the north of the world, the woods of the barrels in which we'd borne water through our journey would forevermore carry the traces of the pure cold springs of New Zealand they'd once contained. A ghost of water. I wanted to be able to carry the character of the country in a bouquet of its scents and colours and tastes. If we could, we would have traded with the New Zealanders for the light of their clear streams and pure mountains. We couldn't but we took them anyway. Their sunsets were part of our story, just as the arrival of our ships had already become part of theirs. We were, us and them, part of the same story, different verses woven into the same song.

In the dark someone asked, 'How long were they wandering with their fires?'

Four years, reckoned Cowell.

They moved on a slow current south, drifting like a continent. They moved like species of trees, like the slow spread of seeds. In some places they stopped for months at a time, planting and harvesting crops on land loaned to them by friendly tribes. Over the years of their southern drift, their women still married, children were born, and their number grew. As they moved they collected the scraps of other tribes in marriages. Warriors travelled with them; these were the charms of Te Rop'raha's travelling war. The land was unstable in those days, the Northern Island moving beneath the shifting weight of dozens of tribes swarming and fighting for land. It moved like a sea, tidal, to and fro. There were some who moved towards Te Rop'raha with gifts of food, and others who moved away from him, afraid of his armed tide. These tribes retreated up their river valleys, waiting in ancestral mountains for the wanderers to pass. Whole tribes left their vast acres of huts and villages empty for months while Te Rop'raha's rising wave poured slowly through. Tribes had learned to alter the angle of their lives in the seasons of war, tending the lives of their old and their children as though they were crops. Occasionally slaughter came, seasonal like summer droughts or winter hail, but when the months of Te Rop'raha's migrant wanderers had passed the people returned to their homes on the rivers near the sea. There they found the traces of the refugees who'd lived in their huts, filling the absences in the houses they'd left behind them. They came upon the blackened traces of fires, grey ashes blown from piles and spread through their cold deserted huts. They felt like ghosts discovering the footsteps of ghosts.

Te Rop'raha's tribe travelled down the coast from river to river, mouth of water to mouth of water. They passed through claimed territories, but as they moved they used the press of people against the land around them like a sailor uses the breeze to fill his sails against ocean currents; like the shepherd uses the mind of the dog against the nature of the sheep. When they stopped to plant crops or to take rest beside plentiful rivers the Wolf roamed the hills around them, learning by heart the folds of the land, its secret pockets that could be used as caches for armed men.

Even into friendly territories they were pursued. In one wide and open river valley they camped and waited calmly through the day for an enemy force of Wy-Ka-Taw to fall upon them. When the assault came their own warriors spilled from out of their hiding places in the hills and the mouths of hidden tributaries and smashed the attackers.

After this battle Te Rop'raha made no cannibal feast but instead let his surviving enemies gather the dead bodies of their fallen and take them away. He warned them that he had allies lying in wait to the north, ready to slaughter any enemy they found. He told his enemies that their safest way lay west, that this way lay unguarded. Thus, with a gesture of protection, Te Rop'raha ended the long and bitter war with the northern Wy-Ka-Taw and bought his tribe freedom from their lingering pursuit. He'd caught the enemy as hawks and released them as doves.

That night we heard the story of how the Wolf took his island. It was told to us by Cowell in the dark beside the fire.

Te Ropraha had led his people south till the outline of Kopitee broke away from the coast of the mainland and floated on the clear blue ocean before them. After they'd seen the island trouble began. Their canoes were stolen. They attacked a nearby settlement in return, killing a number of the people they found there, though they found no boats. In the weeks after Te Rop'raha's people appeared, the bodies of dead men and women began washing up onto river banks. Rumours of new wars had been brought to those districts and the tribes there forged resistances against the Wolf hidden inside the offerings of peace. They gave him gifts of food in the same way that tributes are paid to tyrants. Feasts were made to honour him.

On the shore of a small lake, only a few miles north of where we listened on the beach, the Wolf and his family were fed by the people of a tribe who boasted that their arms stretched from the southern ranges of the Northern Island to Kopitee itself. Te Rop'raha listened quietly. After the hour of eating, when darkness had fallen and his people lay sleeping, his hosts rose suddenly and began to slaughter his family in the dark. Te Rop'raha escaped but one of his wives and several of his children were murdered. Through the night a bloody handful of survivors found their way back to their camp at the mouth of the river where it entered the sea.

In the morning Te Rop'raha swore on the sunrise to send slaughter upriver, to fall upon the houses of that lake from dawn till dusk and wipe its tribe from the face of the earth. Tiny flies stirred the calm of the early morning air, and somewhere in the mind of the Wolf, in the quiet corner of a mind almost consumed in grief and fury, he realised how the fate of two peoples had fallen like a white feather floating on shelves of air and come to rest, soundless, on the skin of his brown arm. He felt the gentle weight and fall, the sudden stop of history. For the tribe that was about to be smashed lay not only upriver, where his freshest vengeance lay, but also on the island he had coveted down the years, Kopitee, burning like his heart's desire in the still blue sea behind him. Suddenly, it seemed, the sun had risen with a silent thunderclap on the morning of his destiny. He saw the design of the earth become clear before him, the exquisite and enormous weight of the land and the winds of those tribes that shaped it, that sculpted it and held it. He stood calmly in the centre of this hurricane. That day a tribe would be erased from the world and the Wolf would fill the space left behind with the new people he'd brought with him, the people who'd wandered four years waiting to be delivered from history into history.

He separated his forces and sent war in two directions, upriver and over sea. With his left hand he destroyed houses, burning the people inside them without mercy. With his right hand he launched his canoes and took an island. In the histories of these islands there had never been a day of such sudden terror, such sudden bloodshed.

In the days after Kopitee was taken earthquakes swarmed. Every tribe knew the land had been resettled forever, as though a monster had turned in its sleep, deep beneath the earth, miles below the surface where not even legends of sunlight were told. A continent of travellers had collided into the edges of settled territories and a new tribe had appeared like new mountains. They blocked the sun and changed the courses of the rivers. No longer could the ancient familial streams be fished from or waded within or named as borders. New people had arrived.

The Wolf and his people repaired to their new island for safety. He left garrisons on the mainland and turned it into a theatre of war. The months of fighting with other nearby tribes were constant.

Kopitee was safe though some battles were fought on the very beach we sat upon, defenceless in the dark, huddled around a small fire and listening to Cowell's stories of the Wolf.

He was an entertainment and a terror we told beside fires, but we felt him against us. In the dark we must have been pale. We were only traders. We sought only flax, or barrels of pork, or meat and potatoes. The skins of seals or the oil of whales. We did not want to be part of his engine of war. We did not want to know whose ghosts we were disturbing on that beach. We had only a brace of guns between us. Some of us carried short swords, others long knives. We would have raised them against the darkness if we thought we'd had to. It was not the flax but the desire for flax we would have protected. For that we would have defended ourselves against the dark things we were scared of coming upon, the things we feared in those islands. Yet we were more like the natives than we thought. We understood the Wolf, what we knew of his desire to accumulate and move, to acquire and protect. We thought he would understand us. Though his was a military mind and ours maritime, we were, both of us, traders. We were, he and us alike, translators of opportunity into benefit, drifters driven by acquisition.

Cowell told us that now there was no war fought in those regions. He told us that we sat upon the calmest and most peaceful of beaches and that we could trust them to be so because we ourselves had sailed to them. Traders like us were drawn to the Wolf, and it was traders like us who had made him the most powerful of all the native chiefs. So we sat in his protection which was a protection we'd helped to build. We sat upon his beach, upon the arm at rest against his side, nestled against Kopitee, his calmly beating heart.

'I don't trust it,' muttered the Watcher. 'I've felt it twitching in the night, this arm. I've felt it turning in its sleep, moving in the dark. This beach is all quiet with the footsteps of sneaking native sprites. I don't trust it, this beach. Listen to that quiet.'

And quietly we listened. But out there in the dark all we could hear was the sound of the sea.

One by one we fell asleep. As I drifted off I fancied I heard footsteps, though I knew the sound to be nothing more than the strange ferns that grew, heavy and white as swans' feathers, a little way from us, shifting in the smallest of breezes and padding against a fallen log. Eventually my time came.

I woke to shouts. It was the middle of the night. The fire had fallen to embers and the wheel of stars above me had swung round to a new position. In the instant that I had seen and noticed the new map of sky above me I heard the sounds of the shouts that had woken me, I heard the splashing of water in the sea. I reached for my pile of things, for the bundle where I'd concealed a knife.

This is what had happened. The Watcher had gotten up and walked, in his sleep, towards the edge of the sea. Brown had been the watchman. He'd seen the Watcher walking into the water, and assumed that he had risen to piss into the ocean. After he had been gone several long minutes Brown began to think otherwise. He roused Kirkpatrick who lay sleeping near him and together they raced down to the water calling out for Ed. Those had been the shouts that had woken the rest of us. We rose and went after them and raced into the water still shouting for our lost man. It was a black night with no moon. There was no light but only black all around us. Eventually we heard the Watcher calling back to us from the beach. We emerged from the surf and found him lying on the sand exhausted and soaking and laughing at us. Having wandered into the water and fallen over, he'd half woken and staggered from the sea confused and disoriented. He sat himself down and then woke up properly and realised what had been happening. By the time we had all gathered around him men were laughing in spite of themselves and the fright they'd suffered, and were putting the story back together, as it must have happened. It was then that we realised Kirkpatrick was not among us. We moved back to the edge of the water calling out for him. We listened for his replies but when we heard none we splashed back into the sea beginning to panic and shouting his name in earnest. We searched for ten, fifteen minutes. Twenty minutes, half an hour. We found nothing. One by one or in pairs we returned to the beach. Brown and Cowell were the last to return. We looked to them hopefully but it was

148

only the two of them who emerged from the shadows of the sea. For another hour we scoured the beach, calling out to Kirkpatrick, but gradually our calls became quieter, more infrequent, until at last the men were utterly quiet, except for the Watcher who wept openly. In the darkness we heard him, the small sound of his sniffing tears above the waves. For a while longer we stayed awake. There was nothing to be done and yet sleeping seemed a betrayal of Kirkpatrick. So we stayed awake and stoked the fire again. Cowell said Kirkpatrick might still return, for the natives often swam between the two islands. There was a chance, Cowell said, that he had swum all the way across to Entry, disoriented in the darkness. But we knew he was gone. For once Cowell's words meant nothing to us.

One by one we must have all fallen asleep.

As I lay against the beach I thought of Kirkpatrick's body, lifeless, becoming slowly cold and blue, tossed and gently rolled by the hand of the sea. I thought of his dead hands, his hair, his shut eyes. I imagined him lying face down in the ocean, his body slowly sinking and finding a final resting place that no one would ever know. I thought of him as a small boy laid to sleep in a cot, through the night his mother looking in and checking on him where he lay.

VI.

October

We woke the next morning and found the world changed. Death had come to the beach. It was the first death we'd had on those islands. We'd listened to so many of Cowell's stories of death and war and sacrifice that we no longer had a place for the deaths of our own, the deaths which occurred outside the frames of stories.

The Watcher was quietest at breakfast. It was a morning neither clear nor overcast. There was some cloud about but it was high and the sun spied through its grey ceiling. The Watcher muttered something about how the sun oughtn't be up that morning. A cool breeze blew to us from the face of the sea. The birds sang and cried either side of us just the same. It is part of the strangeness of the deaths that occur closest to us that the whole world doesn't stop but carries on as it has always done. So we sat there and the world carried on around us. The sun rose and we drank tea and smoked. Cowell said again that he thought

Kirkpatrick could have swum to the coast of either island. He looked across to Kopitee as though for a sign of our shipmate upon the far shore. But we knew Kirkpatrick and his small gangly body. We could not imagine him swimming anywhere. Brown said quietly that when the two of them had reached the water in the night Kirkpatrick had disappeared quickly. I felt sick then as I imagined Kirkpatrick's dead body washing up on the beach with the driftwood and seaweed and parts of dead fishes. I wanted to get off that beach.

The Watcher stood and damned the whole place to hell and walked off along the sand in a southerly direction. We watched his slow amble across the flat sand. To a man we felt for him, for we knew he blamed himself for Kirkpatrick's mishap. As I watched him I could imagine that he would walk as far as he could down that beach so we would eventually lose sight of him and he would be gone from us forever. I could imagine him walking away from us and walking out of our lives. His name was Walker, I remembered. In the time I knew him, upon the *Elizabeth*, it seemed always that although we shared a boat and the duties aboard her, he walked his own line in life, a little way from the rest of us, and in a different direction. There was our adventure and there was his mysterious part in it, as though we formed only the corners of each other's stories. We were a backdrop to his own greater and more private drama while he was a small player on our wider stage. Although I had not considered it until that moment, somehow I had never doubted that one day he would suddenly leave us, exiting our story with scarcely more than a glance in our direction, a slight nod and an I'll be off now.

But when he was a hundred yards or more from us he turned and shouted. He leapt up and down on the beach and waved his arms while he called. We couldn't hear him but the message was clear and at once we ran to him. We must have looked a strange field of runners, for some of us were lank and swift while others were portly and slow, but eventually we'd all run or jogged or ambled along till we stood there with the Watcher, huffing and puffing and gazing upon the body of Kirkpatrick lying on its side, on the beach, resting with his head upon an outstretched arm like a pillow, as though he'd been laid to sleep there upon the sand. We stood and stared as if we'd come upon some miraculous fish washed up onto the shore, but after a moment Brown attended to him and declared him alive. He looked white and waxy, as limp as seaweed, caked in grains of grey sand. As Brown revived him he coughed and spluttered his way back to the land of the living and Wall reckoned he must have swallowed half the seawater between us and Kopitee. He stayed pale and quiet for some minutes. He seemed confused, almost as though he was not quite alive. Brown ordered Wall back to our campsite up the beach for a blanket and fresh water. At some point Richardson noticed a dark wet sack lying a few yards away. Cowell went to it and picked it up. He ran his hands over its patterned woven sides and said that it was no mere sack but a flaxen basket made by native hands.

He turned it upside down and dozens of greenish blue fish shaped not unlike salmon poured onto the wet sand beside us.

'A gift of fishes,' Cowell said.

We stood there quietly and I felt a tiny tremor, a faint shudder of sinister meaning, as we beheld the fishes on the sand. Like the shells the morning before, here was a sign we could not read.

Kirkpatrick sat up but the strength had gone from his arms. We saw death in his blue and white face. He scratched his sodden head and eventually his eyes returned to us, taking us all in and recognising us as he began to speak. He complained of a headache. We asked him what he could remember of the night before and he told us how the natives had saved him, pulling him up from the ocean with their strong brown arms. He did not know how long he'd been thrashing in the sea; he remembered only being trapped in the heaviness of water, unable to rise and break the surface for air. He remembered a shadow moving in the water, too small and narrow for a whale but too large for a shark. He described its enormous flippers for us. He tried to swim away from this shadow but swimming became harder till he found that he was floating and gasping at the fresh air, his lungs trying to take it in like handfuls. Then he was hauled into a boat like fishing tackle and he realised the flippers he had seen under the water had been the paddles of a canoe.

'I cannot speak to the New Zealanders but I know the sounds of their words,' Kirkpatrick told us. 'I knew they were speaking to me. I was in strong arms. A warrior's arms they were that held me. And though I was relieved to be out of the water I was terrified to be in the savage boat. I was thankful to be alive and those arms were a joy

153

to me, and yet they held me in terrified grief. They held me and made me lie down and I heard the voices of the New Zealanders speaking quietly to me. That was the last thing I knew.'

We didn't say anything but looked at each other nervously. Kirkpatrick had been returned to us safe but not the same, unhurt but not unchanged. We saw afterwards that he was no longer the innocent he'd been. It was as though he'd been spoken to by angels. We walked back along the beach and made tea. We ate a few biscuits while Brown cleaned and gutted the native salmon that had been left for us. Though some of the men said they weren't hungry, in half an hour our fingers were greasy with the fresh hot flesh of melting fish.

It was after our second breakfast that the unease I'd been feeling all morning and put down to the stress of Kirkpatrick's disappearance suddenly bloomed into a physical sickness. As the day wound on and became hot again I took myself from the beach wandering inland to the shaded areas where I could rest away from the harsh glare of the sun. When I was alone I pulled my britches down and crawled to the little stream and relieved myself into the waters. A moment later I threw up. I spared half a thought for any of my fellows who were at that moment visiting the same little river downstream. I hoped none were filling the ship's supplies of barrels and casks of fresh water. I remember Brown bringing a drink to me. And when I had drunk it I slept more soundly. Occasionally, when I woke, I heard voices. They said I was ill from the sun. I knew it to be something I'd eaten and yet I felt the heat of the day thick in my head as though my skull was a jar filled with harsh liquid or light. I felt that my brains were rocks, unbearably hot. I felt the earth tilting beneath my dozing head. I heard the flies, suddenly crazy all around me as if they sensed the blood about to spill from my ears. They knew the carcasses that the sea brought. The land was suddenly mad, thick with insects flying and biting, even in my sleeping shade.

I woke later, early in the afternoon. The flies had eased though my body and my head felt heavy and thick and light and empty at the same time. I imagined a native fly had crawled into me, passing through one of my ears to lay some egg inside my head, climbing into me through the gap of a nostril to spread disease about my body. I lay my head in the cool water of the stream and tried to flush myself clean again. I let the water into me, in through my throat and nose and ears and I drank and gargled and spat. I washed my face and eyes and rinsed all the dust and grit from my hair. And still I felt that something had passed inside me and fed itself there, a seed or a worm that had taken root in my chest and would not be dislodged.

I wandered back to the camp shortly after I woke. Men told me my colour was not right. Kirkpatrick and I made a fine pair, they said. They told us they already had our graves dug for us.

'We'll bury you both at the bottom of the world. You'll both be New Zealanders,' they teased.

They asked me if I felt like eating. I did not. I drank tea while the other men ate a scanty meal of biscuits and the last of the dried pork we had with us. There was no conversation. I was ill and Kirkpatrick still shaken but it seemed that even the other men felt forsaken, as though they'd been forgotten on the beach. We looked to our vessel moored a ways from us, to the *Dragon* beyond the *Elizabeth*, nearer to Kopitee, and behind her the island itself. Look at that highway out there, Cowell said to us. Our two ships parked upon it. This is a road we sit beside, not a forgotten corner. It is one of the great roads of the world! From here we could follow its wide blue line to Hobart Town, up to Sydney on our long way to India, south round the Cape of Good Hope, north to London. Think of the hundreds of ships upon this road right now, their thousands of sailors. Within a hundred miles of us half a dozen ships are making runs for flax or hunting whales or seals. And they'll come, all of them, to Kopitee.

Whenever Cowell spoke we felt less forsaken.

At about two or three o'clock we saw the longboat coming from the *Elizabeth* to our place on the shore. Clementson stepped from the boat and called to us that Mister Cowell was needed. He said he had brought no further provisions so the rest of us would be better off on the boat again too. We all took the ride to the *Elizabeth*. As we rowed we looked back to shore. We saw how small we must have been, how visible, on the beach. Our shining bodies and our linen shirts. Our fire. The small ring of churned sand we'd left behind. A small abandoned city or the wreck of a nest we'd left there. The traces of four small walls. And when we turned around we saw Entry even bigger than it had appeared from the shore of the Northern

Island. A sea-monster of land with its bush-clad sides and armour of scrubby trees and ferns becoming knowable to us as we approached. We could feel him there. We were a satellite held by a force, drawn to him and yet keeping ourselves from him.

We arrived at our brig and boarded her.

We sailed over to Kopitee as the afternoon wound on and moored not far from the *Dragon*. When I felt the roll of the deck again it was a source of comfort to me. I knew the feel of the waves underneath those boards like I knew the feel of my own bed or the pattern of my breathing. There was an animal mind in the ocean and I felt calmer against it, reassured by its buffets against our boat, gentle and heavy as a cow's, the character of muscles shifting in the watery back we rested upon and slipped within. But though I was settled by the spirit of the sea a fever still crawled inside me. The afternoon had gathered up all its heat and when we stopped and anchored ourselves just out of Kopitee's shadow it crashed upon me again.

I broke into a sudden sweat and was violently ill over the side of the boat. As the afternoon stretched towards evening I was cursed by foul odours. I tried to ignore them and took to working the decks instead, scrubbing them with a brush and pail of soapy grey water. But as I toiled I smelled the thick stink of manure and carcasses, sour milk and rotting vegetation. I asked the other men if they could smell the strange scents which plagued me. They said they could not. They were quiet towards me and gave me a wide berth as though they feared that my delirium might be infectious. Though I knew the fumes all

around me were phantoms I thought of them as ravens.
And though they must have been some side-effect of my
sickness I thought they told of some river of blood to come;
somehow I was sure that my malady and my madness
were tuned to a sudden change in the season. I felt it in
my bones: that the way we'd had the whole country on
a leash, at arm's length from us, was about to change. It
was about to turn, that island, and begin leading us. As we
lay there moored just beyond the edge of Kopitee's wide
black shadow I knew that we were about to roll beneath
its great weight like a canoe in capsize beneath the weight
of a black wave. Behind us the days had been made of the
rain in our faces and the cold in our fingers and toes, and
though we'd endured the tail of the New Zealand winter
it had been a season we'd worn like a cloak. We'd travelled
safely through those months. We'd had no deaths. We'd
had neither fights with the natives nor misadventures with
the brig. But we'd not yet encountered the mad spirit that
stalked the land in its blazing heat and I was afraid of the
fierce summer waiting for us around the corner of warm
October breezes. In a vision inside my mind I saw the days
ahead made of a madness of blood and a thickness of flies.
A surge of savagery was welling in the land and though it
had been contained by Cowell's stories now it threatened
to tear aside the veil. I felt as though I'd become an
animal and could smell the rhythm of nature, the future
of the shaky earth. I could smell the currents of blood
in the ocean like the smell of smoke upon the unstable
isles whose shifting wet ribs we were anchored to. In this
strange knowledge, with my head as empty as a tipped

bucket, labouring under a dizziness so strong that I felt my soul was trying to escape my very body, I scrubbed the decks furiously in my fever, straining to remove the stain of foul air that had sunken into the boards of our boat. I was gripped by an uncanny certainty that handfuls of blood had spread and seeped deep into the deck. I knew there were no such handfuls and yet still I scrubbed. I saw myself wiping away the stains of spilled claret before it had fallen there, trying to erase an echo before the hideous voice had even sounded.

The sun shone on my hand holding the brush against the wide flat wooden palm of the *Elizabeth*'s deck. My skin had a glow about it. A fly landed on the knuckle of the thumb and in the bright light I saw its shiny wings and eyes, half a dozen shades of green and blue in its blackness, the same shiny blackness I saw on Kopitee. I thought the fly must have come from the island. It could have been a little shard of the same rock from which Kopitee was hewn. Or perhaps the Wolf had taken the shape of a fly and come to us in disguise and sat there, eyeing me, taking my measure. This little monster, this little demon, which sat only a layer of skin above the blood and flesh and bone of my hand.

The New Zealanders of Kopitee Island paddled their canoes out to meet us in the evening. They circled our ship. One of them, a tall man, stood in the prow of his canoe and held a large basket. He hurled it to us on our deck. We opened it

159

and found another gift of fishes and the men made a show
of cheering and smiling and calling out our thanks to him.
He cried back to us some words of blessing or farewell in
his own language and his canoe was paddled away.

'Was that –' began Richardson.

'No,' said Cowell. 'That was a lesser chief.'

I stood with the others in the fresh evening air watching
the New Zealanders return to Kopitee.

My fever of that afternoon had left me as quickly as it
had arrived though it had taken half my weight with it. I'd
sweated it out in my cabin, sleeping fitfully and delirious
till I'd woken around six o'clock with a sudden cool calm
all over my body. I felt like a ship that had come through
a storm. My timbers creaked and my sails were torn but I
was upright and seaworthy. I leaned against the rail and
asked Cowell what had happened during the afternoon
when I'd been below deck shitting into a small tin bucket.
Casually, he told me that he and Stewart and Clementson,
with half a dozen others, had been ashore at Kopitee.
There had been no fanfare. They had taken no extra arms,
no precautions of any kind. Quietly, easily, they'd rowed
to the island and the Wolf had spoken briefly with them.
After this meeting our men returned to the brig.

I tried to contain my surprise but in truth a gulf of
disbelief had opened inside me. I did not understand how
they could have stepped so calmly over the threshold of our
everyday, into a moment of history, and then so easily step
back again to the routine of the ship. Though we had all
seen New Zealanders before – though we'd slept with them
and eaten with them, traded with them and exchanged

clumsy words – none of us, not even Cowell, had come face to face with the Wolf. I asked Cowell which men had gone ashore, which men had seen him, for I expected to see them changed in the same way that I had seen Kirkpatrick changed after he'd been nearly drowned and then saved by the natives. I expected to see the experience written in their faces, an otherworldly light in their eyes. But the men who'd gone ashore were not men like myself or Richardson or Kirkpatrick, or men like Brown or Wall or the Watcher – men who'd listened to Cowell's stories about the Wolf and knew his place in the drifting history of these islands. Stewart and Clementson had no regard for history. Wilson and Jones and Smith were big quiet men, not oafs or scoundrels, but hard men chosen to lend the shoreward party a presence. Davis and Leonard and Adams were sailors I did not trust. These were the eight who'd gone to Kopitee with Cowell. To them Entry was another trading post; a trip ashore meant another load of native flax in the offing, whereas I carried my excitement and trepidation like Richardson, who'd leaned over the rail to look at the tall native throwing his sack of fish onto our deck, hoping to witness the Wolf himself standing proudly in his canoe below us. If men like Richardson or myself had seen the Wolf, the other men would have seen it in our eyes. They would've seen that we'd known something from beyond the edges of the world, that we'd been touched by a beautiful native madness. Instead, the men who'd gazed upon the Wolf were as unchanged as if they'd been grazed by the gentlest of sea-breezes. I was left bereft and empty, adrift without direction.

I was quiet as Cowell and I watched the New Zealanders' canoes reach Kopitee and then, as though he had reached into my mind and grasped the shape of my thoughts, he said quietly, 'He has a mighty face.' A little surge went through me, made of excitement and satisfaction, of equal parts fear and arousal, the more tangible for being felt as an echo through Cowell's words.

'His eyes pierce the soul,' he said. 'And his voice is quiet. Quiet like steel.'

Cowell described the Wolf as I'd longed to hear him described.

He had a nose hooked like a Roman's and a curled lip, curved like an eagle's beak. He had been calm and quiet and unsmiling. He'd stared at Stewart unblinking, gazing without flinching at our captain who'd stood before him while he himself sat, wrapped in a blanket despite the warmth of the day, listening attentively to Cowell's voice in translation as it made our claims upon him, laying down our offers of trade, explaining our interest in his flax. Clementson offered gifts from us, a few blankets and a barrel of gunpowder meant as a gesture and a sign of our desire to conduct business together. When Cowell finished speaking the Wolf did not move or take his clear and terrifying eyes from the face of Stewart but sat for a minute in silence before replying briefly, through Cowell. He told our captain that he had an offer to make us, a proposal, the terms of which he would make clear when we returned to the island tomorrow. Then he rose from where he sat upon the ground and showed great concern for our wellbeing and asked us if we had all the provisions we required. Did we have enough food? Had we all the fresh water and supplies of fish we needed? He made it clear we were to think of ourselves as his guests; we were to come and go from his island as we pleased. His potatoes were our potatoes, his streams our streams, and his women our women. Tomorrow we would hear his offer for trade between us.

I felt quivers of excitement passing through me, a light-headedness. We sat at the edge of a destiny which now lay so visible, so near to us, a faint echo of our fate contained in the shape of the island whose dark side we lay against. Slowly we were entering that shadow, as the sun dropped behind Entry, just as we were slowly making knowable that dark unknown corner of the earth; as one by one we would each pass over to that island and become part of it, as Stewart and Clementson and Cowell had gone to it, as the other men had gone to it, and as the others among us waited to go to it for the first time.

⎯⎯⎯⎯⎯⎯⎯⎯➤

For most of that month we lay moored off Entry, coming and going between her and the boat. We roamed like rats and spread like seeds. We lay with their women, we brought them back to the brig. We took care with their warriors, moving carefully among them, mindful of improprieties and misunderstandings. It was an island of tigers, beautiful and dangerous.

Among these Clementson moved like an old animal of prey, like one that was going blind but could still follow the

163

scent of the women which led him like a piece of string, like a leash. He was helpless upon it. The younger men all watched him, some with brown skins some with white, but all watched him, equally amused. We recognised the common animal alive within us, alive in us and the natives alike. While we watched our chief mate from one side, his foolish and heartbreaking attempts with the local women, we saw the natives watching the theatres of exchange from their own vantage points a little way away from us.

In little clearings near rivers, on the beaches, near their huts and houses, anywhere there was common traverse, Clementson was forced to approach his targets in front of an audience. He would take his hat from his head and clear his throat as he walked towards groups of women. As he wandered on a casual approach we could hear him, his nervous voice reciting quietly the sole native phrase he'd learned, the bauble of strange language he'd polished under Cowell's expert instruction. He would go to a woman who'd taken his eye and offer his New Zealand words timidly, respectfully. Invariably shock or amusement would follow, the native nymph rejecting him and moving quickly away. Clementson would retire to our group and bark some command, blocking out his embarrassment by issuing us with orders. But he could not hide how crushed he was. Occasionally after such an exchange I would catch the look on his face when he thought none were paying him any attention. He was a scoundrel, but when I saw him forlorn and alone I felt badly for him. I do not know if he ever realised that the phrase Cowell had taught him was not the one he'd wished to learn. Clementson had been trying to tell the women how beautiful he had found them, but Cowell had taught him, perfectly, how to say, 'When I open my mouth, pieces of shit fall out.'

<hr />

Why were we there for nearly a whole month? What was it that kept us? We were not there to chase the native women for want of something better to do. We were not there for idle pleasures. We were there to trade. And yet in that month we had none. For almost four weeks we rested as guests of the Wolf, Te Rop'raha, while we considered his offer, his proposal for our business together, settling our terms and agreeing to conditions. We'd come for a load of flax. Cowell and Stewart had calculated a generous payment for seventy-five tons of flax bales. We were prepared to pay handsomely in muskets and powder, in rum and flints and tobacco. But Te Rop'raha was not interested in any of these. He listened attentively to Cowell's offer before patiently turning it down with a cultured wave of his smooth brown hand. Stewart and Clementson were confused and dismayed. The captain fretted that he had nothing else to offer, and Clementson began to swear that the native chief was a vile trickster. But Cowell ignored their ignited tempers and instead calmly asked the Wolf, what did he want? And Te Rop'raha quietly, casually, said to Cowell that he wanted the *Elizabeth*.

So. This was the offer Te Rop'raha made to us on our second day. Cowell related it to us that night, those of us

gathered in his cabin once more, our familiar little family
of listeners shocked into silence by what we'd just heard.
Except for Cowell, none in that cabin had yet set foot upon
Kopitee, or looked upon the face of the Wolf, or walked
upon the shores of his island. We feared for our safety
for then we knew we lay in the water next to a monster
readying to take us in his powerful jaws and snap us in
two. We lay like a morsel to be picked off, a floating cask
of raw meat. We asked Cowell if Stewart planned to sail
that night, under cover of darkness, before the Wolf sent a
flotilla of canoes to attack us and take our brig. We knew
Te Rop'raha was well-armed with muskets whereas we
were only traders, sailors on a peaceful mission. We knew
that if he wanted our boat he could have taken it easily.
Richardson was on his feet. Kirkpatrick was sitting and
turning pale. The rest of us were frantic and anxious. Only
Cowell was calm and, with the ghost of a smile at the edge
of his mouth, he told us that although the Wolf wanted
our boat, it was passage he sought, not acquisition. Te
Rop'raha did not wish to buy our brig, or to steal it, but
only to hire it. He wished us to become a ferry and carry
him to the Middle Island. When Cowell smoothed away our
fears we were as amused as we were relieved, and as we sat
down again we smiled, laughing sheepishly at ourselves
and each other. Cowell said in mock disgust that we were
as nervous as kittens.

He was joking but it was true. We were easily spooked.
In an instant we'd felt the Wolf's designs become suddenly
threatening, like storms at sea that blew up quickly on
clear blue days. When Cowell said the Wolf wanted our

ship, the first thing we felt was danger, and so we saw that, deep in our hearts, we feared him. During those confused seconds there was no moment in which we thought our blossoming friendship with him could sit happily with his bizarre request for our entire boat. Our first impulse was to believe in the darkness in his heart. In those islands we believed in monsters. And then just as quickly we saw how foolish we'd been. We felt like children, frightened in the dark by a ghost story but woken the next morning in a world made ordinary and unthreatening again. We laughed at ourselves and cuffed each other about our heads and shoulders.

So the Wolf had taken a fancy to our ship and to us, her crew. We were to sail the native chief to a coastal region of the Middle Island where he had some business. When that was done we would sail him back to Kopitee. For this service we were promised fifty tons of flax. Fifty tons! It was the highest price imaginable for what wouldn't be more than a fortnight's sail, even in bad weather. We toasted one another – the luckiest traders ever to sail to Kopitee; and we toasted Cowell – the finest trading master ever to make a deal with Te Rop'raha. We even toasted Stewart – a drunken fool whose incompetence and incivility, though great, had not been enough to spoil the trade. That night we drank in high spirits. There was no question we would accept the Wolf's offer: a belly full of flax for a few days' jaunt. None of us thought to ask Cowell why the Wolf, rich in enormous sea-going canoes, would need us to take him south. Later we heard.

But that night we were full of the Wolf. As we drank

more and more we were filled once again with a mad joy for him. We were intoxicated by his savage and noble spirit, and we drank to the way the Wolf had been woven for us by Cowell's stories. In my mind's eye I saw Cowell cavorting between us, a hat or a pail swung in his hands, a haversack full of words slung over his shoulder which could be drawn from, its contents arranged like shells on a beach, cast upon the shore in the shapes of fishes where they could be said to reveal the mind of a strange author. I believed Cowell carried words within him which could show the edge of a mind whose purpose was not meandering but meaningful, taut and powerful as a sail filled with a belly of wind. I knew Cowell was a teller and translator of stories and though I knew his dark purpose lay somewhere in his acts of translation, I could not clearly make out the shape of his mind; invisible as the wind I could only see what it had left behind. I had only whatever poetry and stories had become tangled up in our rigging, born of our dreams of trade, and whatever had been washed up on the beaches of these islands, these drifting scraps of land we sailed beside and tentatively ventured upon. The land was meaningful for the riches we wished to trade from it, but the land needed to be spoken for us, articulated in a northern language we could understand, its rhythms translated, its mind revealed. The carcasses of fishes whose dead bodies had been deliberately cast ashore seemed strange omens to us, for they were only carcasses, could only speak to us of death and survival. But extended as gifts they acquired a meaning, they became currency. They became a handshake between our white English hand and

Te Rop'raha's brown New Zealand one. But it was Cowell who was the sensation of touch between them. Cowell translated skin into greeting, turning flesh into language. Cowell was our breath, the air in our lungs.

His stories had a way of starting somehow far away from themselves, of beginning with their thinnest and most distant edge. So that night when we asked him what it was like to walk on Te Rop'raha's beaches he began by asking us if we had ever walked across English meadows, or over the Scottish and Irish fields that had once been bogs, the fens that had been used as moats or borders, the bracelets of thanes. Had we ever stepped upon those unmarked burial grounds concealing the shafts of ancient war, where fossils of old Angles' battles lay and became poetry, slowly petrifying towards a state of lore? Heads of arrows which had fallen wide of their mark, or else lain lodged in a slain man's thigh till the flesh had fallen away, sinking through the mud to the layers of graves where wood of shield sat beside wood of prow, the worm-turned posts of mead-halls, the spokes and metal rims of wagons' wheels. Half-jewels, those remnants of a savage craftsman's care. Imagine the traces of strange roots and vegetables growing there, in those fields of peat, in those forests of younger trees, whose woods now grow to be cut down and sawn into boards, made into the floors of boats bound for Southern Seas.

Now we sit in the hand those timbers have made, in the palm of the wooden cradle called *Elizabeth*, her fingers of masts standing straight but quietly creaking over us, in waters that the Wolf once crossed in canoes and then

defended against canoes. We sit only a little way off the
beach where, under the cover of darkness, a hundred
canoes carrying thousands of warriors once landed
to attack the Wolf in the last days of his southern war.
That was the last alliance of tribes forged to fall against
Te Rop'raha.

From the vast regions of both islands they'd come.
From the south of the Northern Island and the north of
the Middle Island they'd travelled and gathered hidden in
the forest valleys near the coast. There they'd waited for a
moonless night. When it came, after midnight they made
for Kopitee's wide northern beach. But somewhere on this
island must have perched a lookout who saw their swift
black shadows speeding over the dim silver sea towards
him. In the calm night he heard the sound of three
thousand oars dipping into the sea, and the sound they
made was so sinister, so small and gigantic. He must've
peered into the east as black as pitch and strained to make
out the shapes growing, the darknesses within darkness
creeping towards him, a black net slowly flung from the
shores of the Northern Island. He must have sensed the
assault coming to him over the quiet waves. Perhaps he lit
the alarm fires to wake the island and unloaded a musket
into the air, perhaps he ran down to the beach and raced
alone across the sand, a spear in his hand, into the enemy
hordes as they swept onto the island in the darkness. He
would have been killed on the teeth of enemy spears. The
first to fall in the battle, he would have fallen alone, his
body churned into the sand, trampled and torn beneath
thousands of feet, hundreds of hurled spears and fallen

stones as the invaders hit the beach and the Wolf's army, the tribe of war, met them and held them there. The whole battle was fought through the night, on the beach and up into the steep surrounding hills which looked down upon it.

That night thousands were slaughtered.

Te Rop'raha defended his island against the marauding thousands with only seven hundred men.

In the morning when the sun rose over Kopitee its northern sandy edge wore a shining rim of salty blood. On the beach the invaders sat huddled. They watched as their captors made bonfires before them and when they heard the wood snapping in the heat of raw flames they imagined the sound of their own bones cracking in those nests of fire. They knew as they sat upon the beach that they sat upon their deathbeds. One of their chieftains struggled to his feet and begged to be saved. He was related by marriage to one of Te Rop'raha's nephews, the young lion of a chief whose name meant The Morning Sunbeam. This young chief ordered the prisoner to be released. Then the two of them walked along the beach, talking of families and wars and watching men stoking the bonfires to burn higher and higher. Without warning The Morning Sunbeam turned to the man he had just spared, lifted him by the throat and threw him onto a bonfire. As the victim screamed, mad with pain, he leaped and danced and flipped and tried to find a way out of the flames, but the men around the bonfire tended their fires with long hardwood stokers and they thrust him back into the blazing cage with the points of their fiery sticks. He was roasted alive.

After that death all other prisoners were released, peace was made on the beach and the bodies of the dead were cremated. So the Wolf, this Southern Napoleon, had come to the island like a nightmare and a scourge and yet he'd brought peace in the space behind him. When you walk on his beaches you feel it, this heavy calm in the air, the weight of it held in the wake of some bloody savage war.

Te Rop'raha's famous victory on Kopitee was won in 1824 or 1825. It secured his hold on the vast southern regions of the Northern Island; afterwards his tribe sat like an anchor, dominant and immoveable. From then on his neighbours began to send gifts of food to him, or young girls to become his young men's wives. From even further away they began to send their flax, receiving in return yearly gifts of tobacco and rum and blankets, jars of pickled delicacies, or flints and guns and powder. He became the point of exchange between New Zealand and Britain, controlling all flax to go out and every musket to come in. Traders said he had the ferocity of a savage and the mind of a European.

They gave us more gifts. Cowell acquired a native spear carved from a single piece of hard dark wood. There was no piece of hammered steel nor shard of sharpened stone fashioned and fastened as a blade, but the whole head was carved into the likeness of a fearsome face, with wondrous coloured shells making the shapes of wide eyes. The wooden blade was a long tongue, flat and wide and sharp, protruding from an open mouth. We looked at this thing that had the power of looking back at us and felt a restless spirit moving within it. I held it and it was like holding an animal, an eel, sleeping but alive. Cowell explained that these spears were carved to represent ancestors, that an enemy struck in battle with one of their carved tongues was struck with the power of a curse, with the words of a forebear long since ascended to their pagan heaven. Thus the gestures in war carried a force equal to words.

We received fishhooks and clubs made from whale bones, those white and grey sea-timbers that were washed up on beaches. Bowls and treasure boxes carved from wood, the native timbers which Swann was especially interested in. He ran his hands over the grains. Flax baskets. We were taken with them, with their strength and lightness, their green colour that shifted with the light.

'Imagine whole sails made of the stuff,' muttered Gunn.

Jewellery made of green-stone. Pendants carved into deities whose poses we couldn't understand. Nose flutes we couldn't play. Treasure boxes whose sacred emptinesses left us to treasure the boxes themselves. The feathers of native birds that reminded us of the English varieties we remembered for the differences we saw between them. The combs the New Zealanders gave us, combs like those we saw worn in their dark tresses, reminded us of the sheen of our sweethearts' hair we'd known at home.

They gave us gifts but the Watcher coveted more. He wanted a native boat.

'Twenty native canoes for a ride in the English brig,' he said dryly.

The men laughed but in a quiet moment he explained to me what he reckoned about those native canoes. He said he could see them in London.

'Museums,' he said. 'Collections.' He said they'd each fetch a king's ransom, those boats. He spent the rest of our time on Kopitee trying to convince Cowell and Stewart that we ought to be trading for native canoes, for collections of artefacts, for native heads. He did not succeed though he did acquire another nickname; we couldn't ignore that the native word for canoe was 'waka', not when it was so close to the Watcher's other names. So by the end of our trip to Entry the man born Edward Walker had been renamed the Watcher, Ed Waka.

So we passed nearly a month on Kopitee, wandering her steep sides, mixing with the natives, close but not too close, while Stewart and Clementson and Cowell tried to settle their terms with Te Rop'raha. Te Rop'raha himself came and went from his island in flotillas of canoes. Whenever he travelled from Kopitee to the shore of the Northern Island, sometimes for days at a time, he never went with fewer than five or six of his mighty wooden boats of war. Sometimes we watched as many as twenty depart across the strait. Outside of great poetry there could be no finer or more epic scene. On those occasions I wished I were a painter. Instead I have it forever in my mind indelibly etched, the sight of that mighty warrior chief's hand of war, twenty-fingered and creeping, paddling, over the flat shining sea, Te Rop'raha himself somewhere in the throng though I could never make out his figure for certain, such were the number of fierce warrior chiefs in his tribe.

The first time I saw those boats I was among a handful of men from the *Elizabeth* sitting casually in the sun. We warmed ourselves like white lizards on his beach while we watched his canoes dispatched to a beach where there was no war, only more calm sun. We marvelled at the display of boats, the sheer power that the Wolf had mustered to take even the smallest of steps from his island though it lay protected by hundreds of miles of rainforests, wide sharp rows of mountains across several vast districts which lay under his control.

'Imagine,' said Richardson, 'if we'd still been sitting on the beach over there when they'd paddled across. Imagine seeing that. You'd think it was the end of the world woken up and come to get you.'

We agreed it would have been a fearsome and terrifying sight. Even with Cowell we were not sure we would have wanted to meet them. We would have preferred to run and hide. We would have felt safer praying to the God we were afraid might not even be listening.

'Even the natives,' said Cowell, 'say the mind of Te Rop'raha is unknowable. Some here call him the Great Deceiver.'

'Lucky we're not natives then,' muttered the Watcher.

The men laughed at him, Ed Waka of the dry humour who dealt in sly, unsmiling jokes, but I wondered if beneath their smiles the other men felt, like me, a silent shiver run through them in the warm air of the quiet beach. I sat privately with my troubles. We did not know why he travelled to the mainland in those days before we struck our deal with him. We assumed it had to do with his business in the south, and we assumed we would learn all we needed to learn about that in time. So for the present I sat quietly with the door closed shut on my troubled mind.

And yet rumours spread. Intrigues were afoot. Questions we couldn't answer passed between us like the traffic we saw moving to and fro between our brig and Briggs's ship. Twice Stewart was rowed across to the *Dragon*. On both occasions he took Cowell and Clementson with him. On one occasion Richardson and the Watcher went with them and on another Brown. After these trips Briggs made a return journey to us. What business did we have with Briggs? What concern did Stewart have with him? Why did he wish to see us? We could only guess. Briggs talked to Stewart in the captain's cabin, away from the sunlight and fresh air, out of our straining ears' reach, though we knew Te Rop'raha had made no trade with Briggs. We'd heard that the Wolf had sought the use of his vessel and we'd heard that Briggs had refused him. We wondered why. We wondered what part of Te Rop'raha's offer to us lay still in secret, unnoticed, yet to be declared or waiting to trip us up. Privately our suspicions grew once more. And yet we saw that even after their talks had broken down, Te Rop'raha had allowed Briggs to stay moored off Kopitee. We saw Briggs and his men still wandering ashore occasionally, filling barrels with fresh water and otherwise replenishing their stores. The Wolf treated all traders generously. He knew about trade. He understood the culture of handsome gestures.

Cowell was the only line, the only link forward to possible knowledge of whatever our fates would be, but he came and went from us more infrequently. October was a busy hour for him. He had come with us as trading master, and now was the time when trades would be made or broken. So of necessity he spent most of his time with the captain and his chief mate. Through that month I worried for him as a parent might worry for a child moving carefully through a world of dubious men. Yet we were, all of us, dubious men. And though I knew he was smarter than Stewart and Clementson, and wiser, I could not help the fears I held for him. I could not stand to think of them interfering with him, of their clumsy rough hands changing the way of his mind, altering the way he looked upon the world. I imagined that they thought of Cowell as a boy who could grow to become like them if they steered him in the right direction, treating him with the necessary abuses. They were hard on him. They'd ordered him harshly about when he'd first joined us at Sydney, asserting their authority over him as though he was an intelligent hunting dog whose mind might prove too sharp than was good for it. He was there to fetch them prizes. He was their Springer Spaniel, trained to be sent into swamps to gather the shot ducks and pheasants whose plump dead bodies had fallen there.

But something in Cowell's youth had already been set and so he sat protected behind his able mind. He spoke other languages. He knew other paths of behaviour beyond those that were coarse and crude and found upon English boats, carried into the windy freezing seas at the bottom of the world, to their mad summers. He carried something of himself deep within himself, at a layer none of us ever saw. The Watcher had imagined doubloons smuggled about his body, hidden riches that could be suddenly revealed in his conversation. Perhaps in our own way, each of us was taken with this part of him, with the possibility of treasures and gold coins which always hung off him and which he showed to us whenever we listened to his stories. But I was interested too in the pockets themselves, in the possibilities of containment they represented. I envied the shape of his mind, the control he had over it. I longed for such a reservoir within myself, for I had seen how his stories were a store of value for us all. Because he was a boy who'd kept his secrets upon him he could be what each of us wanted him to be, he would become a man whose meanings were several. When he bared the shoulders of his knowledge to me, I could imagine my hands upon his smooth skin, my fingers searching and kneading his strong arms. Within his chest was a secret store I wished to reach into. I wanted to cup his beating heart. His limbs and thighs a cage around some secret songbird.

One afternoon a storm blew through and we sheltered in empty huts on the island. That night we lay beneath warm blankets in the smell of the warm dry earth and slept soundly.

I had a dream. I was a sailor on an unknown boat, she was a brig but she was not the *Elizabeth*. In my dream I did not know her name. When I turned from the prow I saw that Te Rop'raha was her captain. That was a doubly curious thing, for although I was yet to look upon Te Rop'raha's face in my waking life in my dream I knew it to be him. He had a great face that terrified and captivated me. I saw his savage dignity, his calm eyes and sharp mind that stared through walls into men's souls as easily as a sea-captain reading the sea. He wore part of a naval uniform – a captain's hat and a jacket with chevrons sewn upon the upper sleeves. It looked European though it signified no navy that I knew. In my dream he spoke to us in English. I asked him the name of our ship and without looking at me he said clearly, 'She is the *Wooden Horse*.' It was only many days later that I remembered having this dream. After I had remembered it I told nobody, for by then none would have believed me.

Eventually, as we neared the end of October, and before we sailed south, we learned the extent of our trade with Te Rop'raha. All our questions had been answered and still we chose to sail into our notorious piece of history. On the twenty-ninth of October 1830, on a calm and sunny day, the *Elizabeth* sailed south carrying Te Rop'raha and a hundred and twenty of his fiercest warriors. When we sailed we knew the Wolf's purpose on the Middle Island and we knew why Briggs had refused him. We knew the danger we sailed into. A week or so before we sailed it had all become clear to us – the part we were to play in Te Rop'raha's scheme and why he had needed a European vessel.

A couple of days before the *Elizabeth* sailed Briggs tried to dissuade Stewart from the course of action set down before us. We were back on the brig, making our final preparations to sail. Briggs arrived in his longboat early in the afternoon. That was the first time I had seen him at a close distance. He was a bear of a man. His hair was curly and light, his eyes blue and clear, and his voice was high but strong. It sang out across the whole deck. He seemed twice the captain Stewart was. He stepped aboard us and quickly regarded the brig, checking her sails and her decks. It seemed he was about to issue us with orders before he remembered that we were not his crew and the brig was not his to command. Still, had he given orders we would have followed them. He seemed a man who was used to being obeyed. He tried to impress on Stewart the folly of our course.

Stewart wandered out into the daylight blinking and reeking of rum. He hardly mumbled a hello to the visitor but stood there and waited for Briggs to show his hand. Briggs said a few words in our presence, something about a word of final advice, before Stewart signalled for him to follow below into the darkness of his cabin. Cowell and Clementson went with them.

They emerged a short time later. Briggs had, it seemed,

been unsuccessful in whatever he'd implored. He strode across the boat shaking his head, cursing and muttering. He climbed from the brig back down into his longboat. We watched his men row him back to the *Dragon*. That was the last time we saw Briggs before the *Elizabeth* sailed.

We waited on the edge of history, waiting for night to fall. We slept on board and I waited for the hour to grow late. I wanted to enter Cowell's cabin. I needed to be settled by the calm sense of order he gave to the world.

You would have heard that he was a monster, the Great Wolf, the Southern Napoleon called Te Rop'raha. But if he was a monster then all of us on those islands were monsters. Cowell explained this to me that night. We were about to pass through the thickness of flies. I told Cowell that I could feel it, the madness in the land rising with the heat of the coming season. I told him I had felt it since we'd arrived at the island, that it had been growing inside me since we'd first spied the coasts of the Northern Island almost two months ago. He regarded me evenly, without any concern, for a long moment. Eventually he asked me what I thought to be a strange though harmless question.

'Do you know where the native flax comes from?'

I told him I was sure I did for I had seen it growing in bushes in swamps near the sea. All down the Northern Island we had seen it growing. We knew that Te Rop'raha coveted flax and controlled its trade. He gathered it in vast quantities from the southern regions of the island and then had it scraped and dressed for barter with ships like ours. Cowell told me of Te Rop'raha's huge numbers of slaves, people from conquered territories who had been spared a gruesome end in his ovens but were now kept as prisoners on Entry or else the surrounding districts of the Northern Island, forced to work scraping and dressing his flax. On these islands, he said, there was no such thing as innocent trade, for whenever a European ship sailed from these islands laden with flax it sailed with a hull bloated on native blood. And because of that we could admire Te Rop'raha for the way he'd controlled his dealings with Europeans, the way he'd used the great shifts and flow of people around him to fashion an empire. Cowell asked me if I thought they belonged to the ranks of the most brutal of all savages, these New Zealanders. They were cannibals after all. Then, without waiting to hear my answer, he waved his hand and looked away, dismissing his own question. He said that savage was only an English word anyway. I saw how we were involved. Whether or not we took the Wolf south with his hundred and twenty we were already traders with native blood on our hands.

This, then, was the deal we made with the Great Wolf: in exchange for fifty tons of flax we agreed to take Te Rop'raha, plus a hundred and twenty of his warriors, each armed to the teeth with musket and spear and club, some way to the south, so that they might land on the eastern coast of the Middle Island. From there Te Rop'raha would launch a surprise attack on a southern chief, a man who had caused great offence, killing not only eight high chiefs of the Wolf's tribe of war, two years before our arrival in

182

those islands, but being responsible too for the deaths of several white men many years previous. The object of their mission was the capture of the southern chief. We knew him as Hara-nui. When Hara-nui had been secured and brought aboard the *Elizabeth* by Te Rop'raha and his men, we would sail the war-party with their live booty back to Kopitee. On our safe return we would be paid what we were owed. Te Rop'raha had already ordered the flax to be prepared so that we could receive our load soon after we were moored again at Kopitee.

During the talk between Te Rop'raha and his highest lieutenants on the one hand, and Stewart, Clementson and Cowell on the other, the safety of both sides had been considered. Stewart raised the chance of pursuit by the southern tribe. Surely they would come after us in what would appear to them the most brazen of kidnaps. Although our brig was far swifter than the New Zealand waka over open sea, Stewart worried that Kopitee would be attacked shortly after the completion of our mission, while we waited at anchor to receive our full tonnage of flax. We had no wish to be cast as the aggressors on one side of a native war. Te Rop'raha dismissed these fears out of hand. It was widely known that the tribes of the Middle Island had not acquired the musket in anything like the same numbers as the northern tribes, of which Te Rop'raha was, by far, the best armed. The southern tribes were still months or years away from gathering the firepower they would need to shake the Great Wolf's hold on his central districts, to unsettle his wedge of empire. Pursuit, our party deemed, was unlikely.

For his part, Te Rop'raha had insisted on his own absolute safety. He would not travel with fewer than twenty of his own men, though he reckoned that a hundred and twenty were necessary to meet with the best success on his southern expedition. This was where the Wolf's talks with Briggs had ended. Briggs feared that with twenty natives, each armed and dangerous, Te Rop'raha could have taken control of his ship. At most Briggs would only agree to taking Te Rop'raha with two of his men south. Though we did not know it at the time, the morning we'd rounded Entry's northern edge and seen Briggs's *Dragon* moored off Te Rop'raha's coast was the morning that negotiations between them had reached their final impasse. Our entry into that scene on Friday the first of October had seemed, to Briggs, timed like a pantomime demon's sudden appearance on the stage, ominous and providential.

Fortunately for the Wolf, Stewart was not Briggs. He raised no objection to Te Rop'raha's terms or his desired numbers, even after Briggs had begged our captain to secure, first and foremost, the safety of his brig and us, her crew. For Stewart, on these islands, trade was the first thing; welfare and humanity were second and third or nowhere at all. So Te Rop'raha stared down Stewart with barely any effort and our party agreed to carry a hundred and twenty armed natives exactly as the Wolf had asked. At that stage what doubt can there have been in the minds of Stewart and Clementson that we were to travel as a chattel of war?

And yet Stewart, like Briggs, had no wish to become entangled in the knotty threads of a native tribal conflict.

184

We knew how bloody and twisted those disputes were likely to turn. They would be as dark and impassable as the land that had begotten them. This was where the Great Wolf had proved himself a masterful trader, a tactician. To Stewart, as he had to Briggs, Te Rop'raha painted Hara-nui as a rascal and a criminal, a coward among whose numberless atrocities could be counted the deaths of white men. Te Rop'raha made little comment on his personal grievance with Hara-nui until talks were well-progressed. Though eight of his highest chiefs had been slaughtered by Hara-nui, Te Rop'raha made hardly any mention of these during the first talks with Stewart and Clementson and Cowell. I did not know whether Te Rop'raha's tactful omission of this detail was a sign of his noble heart or final proof of the devious depths to which his designs reached. We knew he was a friend to Europeans but did this friendship demand such drastic action from him on account of historical wrongs committed against our countrymen?

A little while later in his discussions with Stewart, he disclosed, through Cowell, that among the eight high chiefs of his tribe slain by Hara-nui there was one, Te Pay-hee, who had been especially beloved by the English. Pay-hee had visited Britain, acquiring a store of muskets and meeting with many important and influential personages during his happy time on our ancient island. Pay-hee, said Te Rop'raha, was a man who saw the way the fate of their islands was woven; he knew their children would speak to us in our language as well as their own. Because of this Te Rop'raha had encouraged white men to choose wives from

185

the women of Kopitee. Down the years we would no longer be men of separate islands, he said, but there would be songs we sang together that would never be smashed, even when the New Zealanders were New Zealanders no more. So Te Rop'raha sought to protect his trade by making this gesture on our behalf. And if it sat comfortably with the grander designs he had on the Middle Island, if it formed a parlour, a foyer that made an entranceway to the greater conquests he so deeply desired to visit upon those districts, then so much the better for him. In that case we needn't have concerned ourselves with the politics of blood that lay in wait for the southern New Zealanders. They were as inevitable as history and separate from us in our moment. We were to be a transport and no more. We were to provide a little chapter in a wider story that was moving forward as irresistibly as the stars' slow swing round the earth. And, if we were willing to play our small part, then we would be thanked in a richness of flax. That was all.

Ah, how Te Rop'raha knew the strange and contrary ways of our hearts and minds. And how could we, any of us, tell, as if by way of reply or return, the way of Te Rop'raha's heart and mind? I still do not know. But whenever I think back to the Great Wolf of Kopitee, the warrior chief Te Rop'raha, it is with a deep and profoundly uncomfortable admiration.

Still, we knew we were more than a transport. We were a disguise and a blind. We were a glove and Te Rop'raha was the hand inside. Our sails and timber made a cloak over him, a native dagger. We knew that we would sail gently into the southern harbour, appearing over those horizons and slipping into those waters as calm and peacefully as the traders the southern New Zealanders had become used to as well, bearing presents as signs of goodwill, but waiting like a steel trap with a hundred and twenty hostile natives in our hold. We were a gift of war.

Before I left Cowell's cabin that night I asked him what Briggs had wanted with us earlier that day. I was curious to know what he'd said to Stewart when he'd been ushered away into the seclusion of the captain's cabin.

'Gifts,' said Cowell.

'Gifts?'

'Gifts for the southern tribe. To be carried ashore by a small number of us, a couple perhaps, and laid down before them, while I talk with them and tell them that we have come for their chief Hara-nui, who is alone held responsible for the deaths of white men.' Cowell was quiet for a moment but interpreted my look and the question it made. 'We haven't decided,' he said.

In the dim light Cowell and I looked at a map of New Zealand. We folded it into thirds and tucked the northern districts away, leaving us to study only the bottom of the Northern Island as it reached down to the vast slab of country below it, the Middle Island lying like a canoe across Cook's Straits, spread on the floor of Cowell's small cabin. Banks was a smaller island on this map, floating off the eastern edge of the Middle Island, as Entry was a small chip in the sea to the western side of the Northern one. But the map was wrong. Banks was no island, Cowell assured me, but a peninsula. It was a small branch from a trunk, a

kneecap jutting out from the leg of earth that Te Rop'raha
coveted. He ran his hand down it slowly, the Middle Island,
its smooth skin, its curving side of coast, till the palm of his
hand was laid over its knee. The ghost of his touch rested
there. And in our hold Te Rop'raha and his men would
make a hand with a hundred and twenty one fingers,
waiting to close around a kneecap, the bone in its palm
waiting to be broken.

As we came to the end of our time on the island I was still
to catch anything beyond a glimpse of Te Rop'raha. I had
seen him by firelight from a distance, a figure wrapped
in a blanket making the shape of a small tepee beside the
flames. I had seen, walking on the beach, groups of men
I knew to contain him, but I had no way of telling which
figure among their moving herd was his. He moved in a
constant retinue. So as October wore on I was still to gaze
upon the mighty face. And though I was yet to look upon
it I was sure that to meet its gaze would be to come at last
face to face with the spirit of the very country itself, the
islands that we'd called New Zealand on our maps, not
merely the face of one of its most notorious sons, or even
Kopitee Island, but the breathing soul of a young and
violently waking country whose face seemed to us ancient
and beautiful.

I desired to look upon that face. I'd thought of it often. It
was said that Te Rop'raha's tattoo had been left incomplete.
I loved this idea, for I imagined that he carried the history

of his islands written on his face and so I liked to think he'd left it deliberately undone, as if expecting a future that waited to be written there. Cowell smiled and reckoned matter-of-factly that the Great Wolf would never have his face completed. He admitted it was unusual for a chief of his rank to go about half adorned in this way, as though he hadn't yet earned the right to wear a full decoration, as though he was a minor chieftain still to assert which corner of the earth was his place to stand, but perhaps in Te Rop'raha beat a heart sensitive to dramatic and poetic irony; for leaving his face unfinished had given him the most distinctive face of all. His sign defied the fullness of signs, and his signature, a half-signature, was utterly singular. All across these islands men feared Te Rop'raha, the half-carved.

Two days before we sailed I wandered around the northern end of Kopitee. It was a hike of some hours. I wanted to stand upon the far western cliff which we'd seen from our boat falling sheer into the sea, and from which the island took its native name. The whole island was made of crevice and rock, steep gully and thick rainforest, and my clambering made little headway. Eventually I came upon a path which seemed to drop and wind around the island's northern edge. Though it looked to take me lower and closer to the beach instead of up and way from it, I followed, hopeful that it would eventually bend around the island to the left and from there ascend to the high cliffs. After half an hour the path rounded a rocky outcrop and suddenly emerged in an open space overlooking a hidden stretch of beach I had not seen before.

When I looked upon it I almost shouted at once, for I recognised the figure of Cowell, barefoot on the grey sand seventy or eighty feet below. But I said nothing, for I saw that Cowell was engaged in some private meeting. Near him stood a native, a small man, barely five feet tall. He wore a grey shirt, open to the waist, and breeches torn off around the calves. Like Cowell he was barefoot so the pair of them resembled a couple of cabin boys. They stood about twenty feet apart, the native holding a stick which he shook at Cowell from time to time. It seemed that the man was speaking and Cowell was listening. From that height I could not hear the words, even had I shared his tongue, but I could hear human voices rising and falling in the gusty breeze, their sounds blown to me in pieces like scraps of paper. The sun, which although falling had not yet begun to set, cast the wet sand the colour of steel.

The man put the stick into the sand and walked a few feet, making a dark line in the grey field of the beach. He stopped and spoke to Cowell then continued with another line. Against the flesh of the beach he made line after line, ploughing the sand in huge spirals and wide arcing curves, some gentle as hills, some as delicate as twigs, as intricate as the bones in the wing of a dead bird. Every few moments he stopped to point and gesticulate, as if explaining to Cowell the meaning of the lines he'd made. He wandered the beach in this way for an hour till at last he stood back and threw his stick into the sea. The net of strange lines lay on the beach like the perfect skeleton of a beached whale or the wrecked wooden frame of a huge sailing ship,

190

laboriously remade rib by rib. And then as I looked upon it I saw suddenly emerge from within its patterns a human face, utterly strange and compelling. Miraculously it appeared below me: the face of the land itself gazing back, fixing me with its stare through a skin of sand.

VII.

Dead Man

The *Elizabeth* was away from Kopitee from the twenty-ninth of October until the eleventh of November. Over those days I kept a diary, a loose collection of idle thoughts, caught as they came to me and written as best I could, a filter for the speculations I made on the fate of the brig. For I was not upon her. I had slipped the company of my own crew and remained behind on Kopitee, though in that time I spent only a few days and nights alone on the beach. I was neither hungry nor lonely. I had all I needed for several days. Packets of tea, parcels of biscuits and dried fish. A good half sack of potatoes and some pork. I had a pot or two and a dry sheltered spot back from the beach, a shallow crevice with an overhang of rock. Had I needed I could have approached the natives with my crude handful of New Zealand words and sought more food or better shelter.

I saw the *Elizabeth* sail from a high ridge of the island. I sat beneath a heavy cover of scrub and watched her quaint figure, a small lady on the expanse of waves gently riding away over their white foam. She was not a small brig but she looked so small on the sea. She was a fragile thing sailing south into the frightful piece of history that lay there. She rocked like a little horse on the waves.

The *Dragon* remained moored off the island. All through October she'd stayed there as if she had been a guardian angel, watching the *Elizabeth* with her sails hoisted, her wings folded away, watching. Even now as she lay spurned, ignored and abandoned by us, she stayed and waited, lying, like me, in wait for her *Elizabeth* to return.

For two days I saw her there, watching the little signs of life about her, the men going to and fro upon her decks.

On the third morning she lowered a boat. It rowed to shore, landing a little way from where I'd made my shelter so I wandered across the sand to meet the men as they pulled up their boat. They were not surprised to see me; they'd already spied the smoke rising from my fire in the days previous, and my little camp, though hidden, was not invisible. They were friendly men. They offered me more comfortable lodgings on the *Dragon*. I accepted. I helped them to fill the barrels they'd come to replenish from the streams of Kopitee and then left with them in their longboat, leaving behind the small room I'd made on the lap of the island.

That was the first of November. On the same day, several hundred miles to the south, the brig *Elizabeth* had sailed to within sight of Banks. I heard this later, after she'd returned. I entered it into my journal, along with the other dates of her round trip which I learned after the events:

29th October: *Elizabeth* leaves Kopitee.

1st November: Banks sighted.

2nd November: Anchored in the bay. Gifts sent ashore.

5th November: A shooting party.

6th November: A day of treachery. Departure at sunset.

11th November: *Elizabeth* returns to Kopitee.

I spent the first eleven days of November aboard the *Dragon*, oblivious to the precise movements of the *Elizabeth*. She had sailed into seas of the imagination. As I sat in the longboat, rowed like a prisoner or a prince to Briggs's ship on a bright sunny morning, I saw distant mountains rising out of the flatness of sea, the clear teeth of the northernmost reaches of the Middle Island. We were now closer to those sounds than the *Elizabeth* was. They had sailed far further south, forward into a country which remained behind a blue veil of clear sky and myth. The sides of that land were sheer and darkest green. Its back rose into glaciers and alps higher than European glaciers and alps. I longed to see them for myself, without imagining them in the image of the highest mountains I already knew, but I had made my choice and it could not be undone. So I imagined my crewmen sailing into the land of my imagination, knowing I would not be able to invent for myself what nature had already made.

I looked over the side of the longboat and saw the shadows of swift-moving clouds sweeping across the vast flatness of the ocean. They moved like the echoes of large ships or darting canoes but they left no footprints, no wake of cut sea behind them, so it seemed to me in my reverie that they moved more like the advancing waves of bending grasses pushed through English fields in the gentle wind on hot summer days. At that moment I saw the sea as if it was green and yellow meadows. There ought to be a word for such delirium. I felt I could have stepped over the side of the boat and hiked after the *Elizabeth*, or else turned and walked in another direction till I came back to Australia, or further to southern Africa, round the Cape and north to England.

When we arrived at the *Dragon* I climbed aboard and slipped immediately – briefly, temporarily – into another life, though I've found that all lives at sea feel temporary. This ship was the angel of the *Elizabeth*, and so I passed into her care, living for just a shallow time away from myself and the things I had known, knowing that I would not stay under the protection of her watchful wings forever.

I met Briggs almost as soon as I stepped aboard. I saw then that his men's invitation back to the *Dragon* had been more than a mere pleasantry. Briggs had waited for me. There was some mystery about me that he wanted solved. Who was I and why had I stayed on Kopitee? Had I some disease of the body or the mind? Was I a thief, or a ship's mongrel left behind as a punishment, or because I was not to be trusted? Was I a scoundrel of the deepest dye? Had I intended to lead a mutiny and thus been cast aside? Briggs was wary of me as though I was an animal that might prove to be either wild or tame. He could not place me. In the beginning he measured me with the same low regard he'd had for Stewart. I could see his thinking. For just as a ship bears the name of her captain when spoken at sea, so too a crewman. I was of the *Elizabeth* and so I was a part of her, and if she was captained by Stewart then Stewart and I were one and the same.

I considered lying to Briggs. I wanted him to be sure that I had no sympathies with the captain I'd sailed under. A scene flashed through my mind, a false memory which I could paint and make real before Briggs's eyes, a scene in which I had stood up to Stewart and Clementson and told them I would be damned before I rode with them into the south and God knew what gnashing of native teeth that lay in wait there. But I could not lionise myself like that in Briggs's calm steely gaze. So I told him the truth, meek as it sounded in the telling. I told him that I feared for the safety of our expedition. I told him how I was scared to go for I'd heard stories of native butchery. I expected him to look upon me as though I was a witless lamb, his eyes either softened in pity or hardened in contempt and disdain, but instead his calm remained and he simply muttered, 'Aye'. I felt his regard for me rise.

After I'd met Briggs the mate showed me to a small tidy cabin. I found fresh clothes folded and stowed beneath a bunk. They were unfussy and clean, and in better care than the patched and holey things that I wore. The mate winked and said I could use them if I wished. He left me alone and as I changed I thought about whose clothes they might have been, whose shirt I had slipped into, whose past life I had nestled in beside. They had a smell beyond the sea, beyond the musk of sack and rope which clung to clothes worn over long days spent labouring on deck. There were these traces of another, more personal history woven into their thread which I would never know.

After I'd dressed I went above deck and strolled quietly, familiarising myself with the ship. There was a group of three older sailors gathered at the prow leaning over the rail and smoking pipes. As I neared them they turned toward me and regarded me on my approach.

'Good morning, Jones!' one of them boomed at me, and the other two laughed at whatever joke had just been made. I was confused and told them my name was not Jones.

'Dresses like Jones,' one of the men muttered and he turned away from me and spat over the side of the boat. It dawned on me then that I was wearing the kit of another man. The absent Jones I guessed. I wondered where this man was now, and how it happened that I came to be dressed in his shirt and britches. The men fell silent and crossed themselves. Lost overboard between Hobart Town and New Zealand they told me. I must've turned pale then for the men laughed and teased me, saying they could see that I had brought the old superstitions aboard. They slapped me on the back in good humour and told me that they would get more things for me to wear. One of them led me away to a small cabin and found clean clothes and left me to change for a second time. Moments later, when I reappeared on deck, the men eyed me again, and again as I moved toward them one of them called out to me.

'Welcome back, Davis!' he cried and the other men erupted in laughter anew. Calmly I asked them who Davis was. And then with suddenly grave faces they told me that Davis was the bravest man ever to put to sea aboard the *Dragon*. A heart like an ox, they said, though he'd died at sea, diving into the water to save a man called Jones. And again their laughter exploded all around me. I realised that I had no other option but to laugh along with them, even as I felt my skin crawling inside the dead man's shirt, even as I longed to crawl from that wretched thread like a moth from its chrysalis sack.

Those were men with hard humour. Yet the fun they made of me felt like a baptism, a celebration of fresh water at sea. And like all baptisms mine was accompanied by an act of naming. 'Davis Jones' they called me afterwards, or else 'Davis Jones the Dead Man', or just 'Dead Man'. They never knew me by any other name. They did not ask. The names we carried in those islands covered over and replaced the pasts we'd brought with us and the names that had nestled there.

In the evening I sat with Briggs in his cabin as his guest and we drank rum together, he and I. He asked me which ships I'd been aboard. When I replied that the *Elizabeth* was the first and only boat I'd worked on he eyed me curiously, for I must have seemed an old man to be starting a life upon the sea. He took a troubled gulp from his rum and said he'd been practically born on the waves.

'It's a funny thing,' he said, 'the feeling I've had with me for the longest time; though I've lived almost all my life upon the sea, I believe I've always known that it will be a foreign river that takes me in the end.'

For a moment my heart stopped beating and the blood inside me dropped a few profound and chilled degrees. For the words I'd just heard uttered by Briggs had been the same as those spoken by Cowell several weeks ago, perhaps a couple of months, when he'd confided in me the fear of foreign rivers which he'd carried about his whole life, a constant echo inside him like the voice of God in his head. Though I have never seen a ghost, the feeling I had at that moment was like the feeling that I imagine would rise in me at such a moment of unholy and supernatural terror. It was as though I'd witnessed the passing of a prophecy, made more chilling for the way it had been fulfilled in a manner unforeseen. And I was sure then that somewhere Cowell must have died. Perhaps he had been drowned, or perhaps killed violently, for the *Elizabeth* was now a carriage of war. Either way, I was sure that the land had taken him.

I sat mutely, faintly, while Briggs carried on, explaining and reciting the history of shipping he'd lived and known. He was a man who knew the lineages of the sea, he could trace lines of trade the way the natives of New Zealand could recite whole strings of generations that had lived and gone before. His head held names and dates and tonnages which were lost on me. They spread like the night sky, patternless until familiarity made them seem an arrangement, a vast design of information which could be both entered and carried. But at the edges of his entries I sensed the rounded incidences of stories, arcs of greed and betrayal which I could understand, for I knew something about the depths of human motive. In between lines, shimmering around the borders of his ledgers, making the vast pale pages on which he kept his footnotes of accounts and goods, I found the abstract fields of human want.

He told me of the adventures he'd seen. He told me the story of a ship that had been seized by pirates. This ship had been called the *Cyprus*. While ferrying prisoners from Hobart Town to Macquarie she'd been overrun by the criminals she carried. They were led by a convict called Walker who took up command and renamed the captured vessel the *Friends of Boston*. She was badly damaged in the uprising when her own officers and crew had tried to sink her and escape on the ship's boats, but although she had leaked like a shot bucket Walker and his pirates sailed on. Eventually they arrived at Underwood where other sea-captains suspected them of piracy. In a bold attempt to throw them off his trail Walker invited all his would-be interrogators to a grand party held on his ship in their honour. They used the provisions they found aboard the stolen *Cyprus*. Captain Worth brought his wife on board and Walker spent the evening charming her, giving her gifts of ladies' dresses – dresses which had belonged to the wives of the officers of the *Cyprus*, all of whom were safely locked in the hold.

Briggs had been one of the captains invited to the party. He said he'd met the infamous pirate Walker that very evening. Edward Walker, his name had been. And then a penny suddenly dropped for me and I wondered if this pirate called Edward Walker was the same Ed Walker I had called my friend on the *Elizabeth*. Ed Waka the Watcher with his mysterious past and his eye for imagined opportunities, his instinct for easy wealth. But when I opened my mouth to speak for some reason I decided not to say. I'd felt myself becoming quieter since the moment when it seemed that Cowell's death had been promised or signified in the words my host had uttered earlier. So instead I continued to listen as Briggs went on talking, charting his private history of the men he'd sailed with, the names of the men on the trading crews he'd brought with him to these islands. Eventually he arrived at names and men known to me, men I'd met in passing in Sydney, or in the north of New Zealand, or men I'd heard mentioned in the background of the stories told by sailors of the *Elizabeth* between themselves. Briggs had known men known to Stewart although Stewart himself had been an unknown quantity; the captain of the *Elizabeth* hadn't been to these islands before and so Briggs had thought to keep his own careful eye on him. Nor did Briggs know anything of Stewart's right hand, the chief mate called Clementson. Of all the men aboard us only the supercargo, the young trading master Mister Cowell, had made Briggs's acquaintance before. Cowell, the son of a Sydney twine-spinner, adept in the native tongue, and a capable trader.

'Still a pup though,' reflected Briggs, somewhat

troubled, and so it seemed that Cowell was a mystery even to him.

But a thought occurred to me then, a possibility dawned inside me that I longed to be real: if Cowell had known Briggs in a life before, then the uncanny fear they shared, the vision of their deaths being made at the hands of strange rivers, could have been nothing more than an echo, the sound of a young man parroting an older one. For Cowell was a storyteller whose mode was to hear and retell, he was a magpie, a searcher of bodies for shiny buttons and trinkets he could polish and hawk. He was a trader and a fabler, a dealer in the lives of others. And so I smiled quietly to myself, inside, while I thought of him, the youth who'd moved ageless among us, a child making playthings out of the clothes and words of sea captains and wearing them to suit his own purpose.

In 1828 a chief of the Middle Island had insulted Te Rop'raha, saying that if ever the Great Wolf set foot upon his island then the chief of Kopitee would have his belly ripped open with a shark-tooth knife. Te Rop'raha had already made known his designs on the large Middle Island, openly coveting the green-stone which grew in its rivers, lying at the base of huge mountains in the most obscure regions west and south of the island. The island was called, in the native New Zealand language, 'The Water of Green-stone'; the chief who delivered the threat to Te Rop'raha was named 'Eat the Crayfish'. Though his words were meant as a show of strength, a last desperate attempt to deter the Wolf from making his inevitable assault, once the insult had been offered the Wolf could not take any other course but to demand the full price of blood and land.

Te Rop'raha attacked the northernmost reaches of the Middle Island with canoes and muskets. He ordered his men to paddle out in a wide arc of the ocean and approach the coast from the south, not the north, with weapons hidden in the hulls of his canoes. On the beach watched those who were used to friendly visits from their southern neighbours, and without any weapons of war they paddled out to meet the arrivals, mistaking the invaders for friends. They were slaughtered upon the sea and their bodies washed up onto the beach. Te Rop'raha and his men landed and destroyed whole tribes and sub-tribes. Of the survivors many were taken as slaves, while others the Great Wolf ordered to be let go, knowing they would fly south, spreading rumours of the horror he'd brought to them. He made them messengers. Down the side of the island they carried the promise of his war before him.

In the following months more attacks came till Te Rop'raha controlled all of the northern districts of the Middle Island. Further to the south, closer to the island's green-stone heart, the tribes were stronger, governed by stern and war-like chiefs. Attacks were harder to make. Instead, Te Rop'raha with a hundred men landed in canoes miles to the north of Banks. They marched south along the beaches till they came to a fortress and camped out before it. They said they had come to trade muskets for green-stone. Eight chiefs of Te Rop'raha entered the fortress and eight chiefs were slaughtered. Te Rop'raha escaped. He returned to Kopitee and considered his reply.

In those months he saw European traders peacefully anchored in his bays and watched while his people paddled their canoes out to meet them. He saw gifts exchanged between two worlds, friendships made before larger trades. He saw his people calmly venture aboard. They passed whole nights in the white men's care.

When I reached this island I sailed into another history, said Briggs. I left behind the ledgers and logs which recorded the details of loads of flax, the vast tonnages of whale oil and numbers of seal skins, and instead passed into a language I did not understand. It was old enough to contain me. It would make us part of a song sung by the years of these strange islands' history of bloodshed. I knew that was where the Rapala would sail us. Though I did not share his language I knew something of his mind. Perhaps, said Briggs, perhaps we did share a language, the Rapala and I. For I would have helped him. I would have sailed him south, from Cobarty Island to Banks Peninsula. I would have waited for him to return to the boat with the object of his desire, this southern chief, the monster who'd killed white men as well as brown. But I would not sail with a hold full of natives of war. That would have been to give up my whole ship. To that I would not agree.

It was the evening of the sixth of November that Briggs had shared the corners of his history with me, telling me how he'd refused Te Rop'raha, the Great Wolf of Kopitee, the Napoleon of New Zealand. The Rapala, as Briggs had called him. The Rapala of Cobarty. No matter. I did not try to correct him.

For five days after the sixth we waited off Kopitee. I asked Briggs why he stayed anchored there. His trade with the Wolf had come to nothing and the *Elizabeth* had left as well. But he told me he was waiting there for another ship – the *Argo*, sailing under a man named Billing. He told me that aboard the *Argo* was a man named Montefiore, a trader from Sydney who'd bought land in the north of New Zealand. Montefiore wished to establish a trading station. Briggs wished to meet him. He would arrive at Kopitee in the coming days. So we sat and waited for two ships: one from the north, another from the south.

We had a day of hard rain on the seventh. By the next morning it had stopped and we saw steam rising out of the island's forested sides. It seemed that Entry herself was a burning hot ember floating in the sea.

Days passed
like ships out to sea.

In ships sitting dead
men in waiting.

VIII.

Return

The morning of the eleventh: a clear morning and a small ladder of sails to the south. *Elizabeth*. She appeared at the hip of the country, passing through the straits between the Northern and Middle Islands, wide and tempestuous waters through which I never passed. We saw her appear and watched her approach. The sight of her, the wait for her, made me ill. In all weather I had watched and waited for her and now the sight of her made me sick. I couldn't stand her slow way towards us. She leaned and rocked forward, a knot at a time. In an hour or so she was in our water. I could see the familiar faces of the men I knew. A handful of white faces against the hundred or so natives on deck.

I waited with a hatful of nerves. I wondered what my name had become to them. Was my name now a curse, a word to be taken in vain? I wondered if they knew I had abandoned them. Or would they think that I had been killed, my body fallen while walking in my sleep, drowned in water or dashed upon rocks? Would they rejoice to see me again?

Before the *Elizabeth* had sailed south with Te Rop'raha I had not told any other man that I would not be upon her. I had disappeared the night before she sailed. A number of us had passed the final night upon Kopitee, sleeping near the beach. I rose silently in the middle of the night and wandered in the dark along the beach and then up into the steep hills, through trees and scrub with no paths, clambering up sheer faces of slippery rocks where I left no path and where no man would think to follow me. In the morning the sun rose in red clouds torn against a blue grey sky. I remembered the rhymes about shepherds and warnings in which red sunrises always promise foul weather. They would sail anyway, ignoring the sky just as they seemed to ignore my absence. Shortly after sunrise I saw our longboat row out to the *Elizabeth* and then later, throughout the first half of the morning, several native canoes went to and fro carrying men and arms and provisions and baskets. Their plans would not wait; the native party of war would not be stayed for the sake of one disappeared sailor. Still, I wondered what had become of me in their minds as they sailed away from me, not knowing that I watched them from behind.

On the morning of their return they moored a little way from us, though too far away to hear us call out to them. I was relieved our calls did not carry, but curiously deflated in equal measure. We looked on as men of the *Elizabeth* lowered the skiff and then we saw our captain and a native chief climb down into the boat, behind them a couple of armed warriors with another in chains between them, then another few crewmen. They rowed the boat ashore. Before they landed native canoes had begun paddling out from the island to meet their returned craft of war, their English blind. Over the morning we watched as dozens of natives in chains were lowered into canoes, while other boats were loaded with baskets. All were paddled ashore. We estimated thirty prisoners and a hundred baskets. Before the last of the canoes had landed, Briggs had his longboat lowered and, with most of his officers, rowed to Kopitee. From our distance we could not properly make out what happened there. We thought we saw the natives dancing; we thought we heard their chanting voices coming to us across the flat sea.

Later in the afternoon Briggs returned with his men to the *Dragon*. He seemed much upset and would not speak to us; he would say neither what had happened at Banks, nor furnish us with the details beyond what we'd seen on the beach. I was surprised when he sent for me.

In his cabin he poured two glasses of rum. He smiled nervously, and raised a glass to the safe return of *Elizabeth*. He gulped and said the first thing was good news: I was welcome upon my ship. He had vouched for me. He had told Stewart that I had been found some way from where I and my fellows had camped on the beach. He said a couple of his men had found me dazed and without any memory of the night before. A mystery, he'd said to them carefully, but not one authored by any criminal mind. So, he breathed, that's a good thing. I asked him if he knew what had happened at Banks. He told me he did, but after a spell of silence all he said was that my friend Cowell was the better man to ask. He told me some of my crew were stationed once more upon the island and that I could be deposited there if I wished. He drained his glass which I took as my signal to do the same. I thanked him and took my leave. That was my final night aboard Briggs's ship.

The next morning men from the *Dragon* rowed empty barrels to be refilled on Kopitee. I went with them. I helped them with their labour and then they left me on the beach. I waited on the sand for men I knew.

I walked to the crevice where I had sheltered those first few days and nights after our ship had sailed. I gathered up the things I had left there, my pots and provisions, and made them into a small bundle.

That was where I waited until after midday when men from the *Elizabeth* appeared on the beach. I was relieved to see Cowell there. George Brown and the Watcher as well. I walked out to meet them. I felt as though I was crossing the threshold between death and life, returning to them in that way, approaching them unannounced after my sudden dis-appearance. I did not know what welcome I would receive. They saw me from some distance and stopped where they were on the sand while they watched me moving towards them. When I was near enough to see the looks on their faces I saw expressions of neither joy nor anger, neither surprise nor fear, but overwhelming tiredness. They'd been made old and weary. They'd been hardened. Even Cowell, the youth whose face had been ageless, had become worn with the care and weight of the years. Only twelve days they'd been away, yet it seemed a season must have turned and passed with every one of them.

Still, they managed smiles when I was finally near to them. They offered friendly greetings, but they were not jubilant. By then they'd all heard the story planted among them by Briggs, that I'd wandered off in my sleep, that I'd woken the next afternoon half a mile away, dazed and without any memory. The story had been accepted, strange though it must have seemed to them. There seemed little to say. Clementson said nothing to me at all. But even the others, those I'd considered my friends, Brown and the Watcher, seemed to hold me with a new and guarded suspicion. They were vague and quiet when I spoke to them. My words were ignored, my questions answered briefly or not at all.

I learned that they had arranged to meet a boat sent out from the *Elizabeth*. As we crossed the beach we saw it lowered. We watched it row across to us. I hung near the back of the group, beside Cowell who had not ignored me in the same way the others had. We spoke in quiet voices. He told me the others had all had their superstitions woken. He said they would become re-used to me in time but for now they were still jumpy. His voice lowered further and he told me that as they'd sailed back from Banks the idea had grown that my mysterious disappearance had been an omen all along. They oughtn't to have gone without me. But instead they'd ignored the sign and look what had happened. I opened my mouth to ask, but Cowell cut me off. 'Later,' he said.

210

As we walked behind the others, talking quietly, while they spoke among themselves, we passed over an area of sand which had been much disturbed. I recounted that it had been there that we'd seen, from the deck of the *Dragon*, the native gathering the previous morning. It had looked to us like dancing. We thought we'd heard singing. The men I now walked with had all been there. They paid little attention to the churned sand, the charred sticks in the earth and the burned leaves spread around, the rocks which had been curiously gathered there. Cowell told me that that was where the natives of Kopitee had had their victory feast. They'd carried their meat all the way from Banks. It had been loaded into baskets which had been taken ashore by canoe when they'd arrived yesterday. So we walked through a sandy field of feastly remains. I looked to the ground and saw charred bones already whitening in the sun. What I took to be scraps of gristly meat, small pork chops too tough to eat, lay scattered. I bent to pick one up. For a moment it appeared to be no joint of meat I knew or recognised. And then I realised I was holding the burned flesh of a human finger. I stopped walking and looked ahead of me. My friends were walking leisurely through the site of human repast as unconcerned as if they were passing through a crop. Which, I suppose, they were.

Having delivered Te Rop'raha and his men safely back to their island fort Stewart waited to be paid his due in native flax. There was little for us to do but sit and wait. The Wolf said the flax was not ready but that in time it would be paid to us in full. He delivered this news calmly so calmly we waited. We waited for the rest of November. Our hull remained empty.

Well.

Our hull was empty of flax, but not entirely empty; not empty of native treasure. We had a prize of another kind there. It was several days before I heard of the rare bird we held safely below deck. I only had the whole story from Cowell given to me piece by piece. But after some days going on weeks I was able to understand, for myself, a loose order of events.

On the morning of the first of November the *Elizabeth* sighted Banks. It was not lost on me that that day measured a full month since we had first seen and recognised Entry. And though our maps still lied about Banks, telling us that she was an island and not a peninsula, I felt an ambiguous resonance. There was an echo of Kopitee in her southern counterpart, for the *Elizabeth* had appeared to sail to both of them for peaceful trade, stepping carefully over the peaceful waves.

They arrived and cast their anchor off Banks on the second of November. Everything was quiet. In those sheltered southern bays, said Cowell, the water could be as still as a lake on a day without a breath of wind. They waited on a sheet of green glass. The days were still and hot and full of sand-flies. Stewart ordered a boat to be lowered. A handful of men took ten muskets and two casks of powder ashore in a gesture of goodwill to Hara-nui. A few hours later they returned to the brig. Hara-nui was away from his home, but a message had been sent to him: Captain Stewart invited him to board his ship as a guest and a partner with whom the British wished to trade. The *Elizabeth* was full of muskets and these would be paid for a load of flax. They waited on board for another three days. The sun beat down upon them.

It cannot help but strike me now that they'd chosen to give the southern natives a gift of guns. That our men went to them dressed in peace but offering war. That they extended a symbol of blood and domination that was a promise, of a kind, but also a blind, for the guns they'd brought seemed like omens of their lies.

On the fifth of November a shooting party went ashore for sport. Stewart and Cowell with guns for the shoot, plus four or five of the ship's men, all unarmed. For an hour or two they shot, mainly the fat native pigeons that favoured the high branches of trees where their large, dark silhouettes made easy targets against the light backdrop of the sky. At midday they returned to the beach to take the longboat back to the brig. As they rowed across the wide still bay they saw a native canoe round the headland a little way from them and swiftly advance. Stewart ordered the dozen or so pigeons that lay in the bottom of their boat to be covered with a sack. When the natives drew up beside them the captain fidgeted. In the canoe sat a very great chief. Beside him knelt a young girl, only twelve or thirteen but already beautiful. About them in their boat were gathered a number of their people. The chief was

Hara-nui; the girl his daughter. The two boats spoke to each other and through Cowell Stewart invited Hara-nui to his brig to be entertained and discuss trade. The chief did not answer immediately but asked if our boat had come from the shore. Stewart instructed the trading master to lie. When Cowell said they had not been ashore that morning but had only been traversing the bay, Hara-nui remarked on a bright green burr sticking to the captain's trousers. He asked how it had come to be there if they had only been upon the waves that morning. He smiled and asked Stewart if he kept living trees somehow secretly aboard his ship. The chief grinned like one who knows he has detected the harmless lie of a simple but likeable child. He shared a joke with Cowell that he would like to see Stewart's great trees for himself and invited himself aboard the longboat. His daughter came with him, and three or four of his men. His own boat was paddled away while the crewmen of the brig rowed their live bounty to the *Elizabeth*. Now, years later, I imagine the chief and his daughter sitting calmly in the boat, a few feet away from the bodies of the shot native pigeons that they never knew were there, a little cradle of slaughter slowly rowing towards the hidden teeth of the Wolf, his wooden jaw waiting.

Hara-nui, it was said, was the first man out of the longboat and up and over the side of the *Elizabeth*. Clementson came forward and led Hara-nui to the fore cabin. Behind them followed Swann and a couple of sailors. Hara-nui was unarmed. They all passed into the cabin and then the chief was clasped suddenly in irons. Swann said he did not struggle, but he seemed confused and agitated. His men were led to another cabin, but his daughter was brought to him.

No alarm was raised. None was possible.

Over the next hours canoes from the shore continued to come to the side of the *Elizabeth*. The natives of Banks were welcomed and climbed aboard. There they were led to cabins and secured or else to lockage in the hold.

The wife of Hara-nui came aboard in this way. It was said that Te Rop'raha himself seized her and allowed her to reside captive in the fore cabin with her husband and daughter. Who can imagine what Hara-nui thought when he saw the identity of his true captor, the Wolf of Kopitee, entering the makeshift cell of his cabin, holding his wife in his strong and hateful arms but bringing her safely to him? I cannot imagine that scene.

I have since heard a story that Te Rop'raha brought before Hara-nui the son of his most beloved chief – the man called Pay-hee who had been slain and eaten by Hara-nui People-Eater two years before, and whose unfortunate death had partially begun that whole affair. The story runs that this dead chief's son, a young warrior prince called Hee-kaw, was brought before Hara-nui in his bonds in the fore cabin of the *Elizabeth*. Hee-kaw stepped forward and opened the old chief's mouth with his hands, drawing the lips back to reveal the teeth, and cursed those fangs that had chewed the flesh of his father. I do not know the origin of this story. I do not know how such stories start.

After the visiting natives of Banks had been taken captive, the crewmen of the brig realised that Te Rop'raha planned to go ashore and destroy Hara-nui's village.

Clementson and the other senior men – Brown, Wall, Richardson – swear they went to Stewart and quietly demanded that they set sail straight away. I do not know if Stewart tried to dissuade Te Rop'raha from his desired course, but with a hundred and twenty of his own armed men the Wolf had physical command of the brig. Thus, Briggs's fears had come to pass; Stewart was no longer the master of the *Elizabeth*.

Night fell and sank restlessly.

At about one o'clock in the morning the warriors of Kopitee climbed down into the canoes which the natives of Banks had left empty and tied to the side of the brig. Stewart ordered the ship's skiff and whaleboat to be lowered and manned. The boats landed on the shore in two parties, half at one end of the beach, half at the other.

At around two o'clock in the morning the warriors sacked and razed the village. The sailors left on the ship watched as the night sky over the hills turned red with flames and open blood.

All through the night the butchery continued. A few Banks natives escaped, a few were taken prisoner; most were slaughtered.

At daybreak the boats returned to the brig though most of the victorious warriors stayed ashore.

For the rest of the day traffic passed between the ship and the shore. The houses were still in flames in the hours after sunrise. Throughout the morning occasional survivors were found, possibly maimed and in hiding; they were killed with spears or beaten to death with clubs. The bodies of the dead had their heads removed and were cut into pieces. A feast was prepared from their remains. Holes were dug in the earth and hot stones laid in them. Into these nests of burning rocks green leaves and bleeding flesh were piled in layers and then water poured upon them. The steam was contained by a final layer of heavy mats upon which freshly dug soil was heaped, raised above the level of the ground so the ovens looked like fresh graves marking the earth. The meat that was not eaten that day was packed into baskets and paddled out to the *Elizabeth* in the evening. About twenty prisoners were taken aboard the brig where they joined the fellows of their tribe in the hold.

When all were aboard Stewart ordered a death salute to be fired. Ten guns spoke into the warm air. Then they sailed. That was the sixth of November.

On the eleventh they spied and landed again on Kopitee. The baskets we'd seen the men unloading had been the baskets of human flesh packed at Banks. The prisoners we'd seen escorted to the island had been the people of Banks who'd been allowed for some reason to survive the massacre. On Kopitee they became slaves. They sat bound on the sand and watched while their captors unpacked the baskets and sat to another cannibal feast on the beach.

So we waited through November. The flax took an age to prepare. We received nine or ten tons of our promised fifty before the end of that month.

We continued to wait.

We saw other traders come and go as the spring grew old around us and became ready to bloom into full summer. We wondered if we would see Christmas on that island.

It was a warm and idle afternoon a good way into November when Cowell and I and a handful of others took the skiff to the Northern Island. It was a long and honest row across those miles of sea. When we drew up Cowell and I wandered the length of the beach. We looked upon the miles of flat sand ahead and behind us, and we felt that it was a different beach to the one we'd camped upon only six or seven weeks before. A different spirit hung over it. It had become a part of us, less threatening. The footprints we left upon its sand didn't feel like a measure of our trespasses. Though I still felt distanced from the rest of the crew, I knew we'd all passed over into the lore and care of these islands. This country had welcomed us with its bloody hands. We lay now in its palm.

It was then that I asked Cowell what had become of Hara-nui and it was then that he stopped in his tracks and told me, as if I ought to have known all along, that Hara-nui was still a prisoner in our ship. My surprise was almost enough for me to exclaim out loud, but I did not say a word. Instead, we stood there together in silence and Cowell looked at me while I looked to the brig, lying out there under Kopitee's wing, at the edge of her shadow, and I beheld her there like a floating prison, a wicker cage we'd made for an exotic native bird. The arrangement, Cowell explained, was meant to suit both sides; our captain was assured of his flax while Te Rop'raha could pay his debt at his leisure without suffering any dent to his honour. We were still guests of the Wolf and he continued to extend his friendly hand to us, offering us food and shelter and a place in his bay for our boat to moor and repair.

But as the days stretched on the men became restless. We wanted to leave. As other traders stopped at Kopitee to trade or refresh their supplies our name became notorious. Word spread of the *Elizabeth* and the live cargo she'd run, the prisoner she still held in her belly.

We waited through November.

We waited through most of December.

Briggs waited too. Though I knew that he waited for his man Montefiore to appear with Billing in the *Argo*, it felt to me as though he waited in his ship watching us, still keeping his distance like an angel, watching us from beneath his wings still folded, from underneath his sails still hoisted. We did not know the mind of him. He watched us in silence with his invisible eyes and I imagined he was there only because we were. I thought he would stay there as long as we stayed, keeping a ledger of our movements which would only be read out on our final day.

Stories roamed. Rumours were passed between the men of different ships. We heard that Briggs was keeping a native boy in his cabin. It was said that he'd saved the child from slaughter on the beach on the day that the *Elizabeth* had arrived and the prisoners of Banks had been taken ashore.

We did not know what to think. Some men looked the other way and did not say anything. The Watcher said that he had never trusted Briggs.

⸺⸺⸺

All along the coast of the Northern Island we saw the black green trees suddenly blooming with blood red flowers. Cowell told us the New Zealand name of this tree; it was a string of native sounds that I never learned to handle properly. But it was a beautiful sound, this New Zealand name, a bird call in itself. And although I could never say it, whenever I heard it spoken I recognised it, and I knew it to refer to those black and green trees which bloom blood red in the weeks of New Zealand's high summer around December and January. Whenever I heard it I saw red blooms in my mind's eye. I thought of the festival they made, which were not only a celebration of that country's warmest months, but of the Wolf himself, the trail of blood he'd left, the trail of red cloaks he'd made and laid on the ground as he'd led his people to Kopitee.

IX.

Echo

I was not aboard the *Elizabeth* when she sailed into Sydney,
though I heard she landed there on the fourteenth of
January, 1831. Briggs had arrived in the *Dragon* the
previous week and given such a thorough account of
events at Entry that when Stewart landed he was arrested.
He and Clementson were wanted as accomplices to the
murder of native New Zealanders at Banks on the sixth
day of November of the previous year. Similar charges
awaited Richardson and George Brown and Mister Cowell.
The police took the depositions of Swann and William
Brown, as well as men called Montefiore and Kemmis,
both of whom had taken passage from New Zealand to
Sydney on board *Elizabeth*. But those courts were stuffed
with paper and the warrants took a time to materialise.
When they were finally prepared the crew of the *Elizabeth*
could not be found. News of the bloody *Elizabeth* had
notoriously preceded them. For weeks whispers had torn

through the whole town that the entire crew was to be had for murder. After they'd arrived only Stewart, too drunk to organise himself, had stayed in Sydney any length of time. Eventually, as the months wore on, even the charges against him were dropped. While the legal position meandered Stewart was released and slipped quietly away. The whole affair, the 'incident' as it became known, was consigned as a footnote to history. My name was forgotten.

We heard that Stewart died at sea in bad weather as his ship rounded the Cape. We heard that his body, a sack of old bones reeking of rum, was turfed into the ocean by his crew without ceremony.

Towards the end of December Stewart, tired of waiting for Te Rop'raha, had handed Hara-nui over to the Wolf. At that stage we had received about seventeen tons of flax. We probably would have received more had we waited but Stewart's nerves had been wrecked. By December none on board would talk with him unless they had to. He knew his crew despised him and he must have known that most others thought him a fool. When Briggs arrived in Australia he loudly declared that he had implored Stewart to keep the chief Hara-nui in his protection and to transport him to the safety of Sydney. There were others who said they had advised Stewart the same way. Perhaps surrendering Hara-nui to Te Rop'raha was Stewart's final sad attempt to reassert himself as the master of the *Elizabeth*.

Whatever, around Christmas Day the Wolf received his prize, the gift of a southern chieftain, and Hara-nui, who'd been born of the highest line of the ancient chiefs of The Water of Green-stone, was betrayed by the man from Yarmouth who'd sold his ship and his soul to Te Rop'raha, the Great Wolf of Kopitee. There was little ceremony. It was a simple matter. The mere lowering of a boat.

There were a few of us on deck when Stewart ordered Richardson below to fetch Hara-nui in chains. We thought nothing of it; by December our security had become lax and the chief was allowed on deck for fresh air each day, sometimes in chains and sometimes without. He was an old man. He could not have escaped. So Stewart ordered him to be brought out from the fore cabin and into the daylight. When the chief appeared he was steered down into the whaleboat. Cowell and a few others rowed him to Entry. Stewart said nothing but watched them row for a bit and then went to his cabin. It was such a small and casual moment that we did not realise what had just happened. Montefiore it was who came above deck and told us that Stewart had just said that he'd released the prisoner for good.

An hour or so later a canoe came out from the island. It stopped by us briefly. We saw that Hara-nui and Cowell were both aboard. Cowell called up to us that Te Rop'raha was not on the island, that he was on the mainland and so Hara-nui would be paddled there. We saw the respect in which Hara-nui was held even by his enemies, the men of Kopitee who paddled him in chains. Montefiore was anxious to be let down into the canoe and paddled with them to the shore. We let him go. As we watched the strange party paddle to the coast of the Northern Island I was sure that Montefiore was hopeful of a chance meeting with the fearsome native trader, Te Rop'raha, our Great Wolf.

He was still a mystery to us, was Montefiore. He had arrived in the *Argo* a few days earlier with Kemmis, his business partner it was said, also of Sydney, with whom he'd bought land in the north of New Zealand. By the time the pair arrived at Kopitee, Briggs, who'd waited six weeks for the *Argo* to appear, had tired of waiting any longer and had already departed for Sydney. The *Argo* was only stopping at Kopitee for fresh water and so the two traders took passage with us instead. They were keen, Montefiore and Kemmis, to make the acquaintance of the New Zealanders.

We regaled Montefiore with our stories of the Wolf. We told him about his terrible eyes, his hooked nose, his calm voice as strong as steel. Montefiore was eager and nervous to meet him. He demanded instruction from Cowell in the matter of the correct pronunciation of the Great Wolf's native name. We saw how our visitor made a show of attempting to produce the sounds of the New Zealand tongue with the appropriate cadences and we listened to his attempts fall hopelessly astray. He called Te Rop'raha 'The Rass-araha' in hushed tones of religious awe. It irritated and amused me to hear the Wolf's name so badly abused, though I knew the exact sound of it evaded all our attempts at replicating it.

Once, as we'd walked in the forests of the Northern

Island, Cowell had spoken its syllables out very slowly, laying them down in short hammer taps for me to follow: te-ro-pa-ra-ha. While I tried to make a string of those sounds Cowell listened and thoughtfully plucked a widely splayed native leaf, the small black-stemmed branch from a bright green shrub. He said this plant was called pa-ra-ha by the natives. Paraha. It was not quite the convolvulus leaf, not quite the leaf whose name the Wolf shared, but it was one similar sounding. It was of the same family of plant, of the same family of word. Cowell held the paraha leaf closely and ran his fingers along its delicate green edges. He remarked how they folded in waves. Like the sides of a hound's tongue, he smiled.

For years afterwards I cherished that common little fern; for uttered in its own language its name echoed the true name of the Wolf, while its leaf, shaped like a dog's tongue, recalled the foreign totem we'd given him. Te Rop'raha's names were spirits and invocations of his character, of the way we'd entered and moved about his islands. When I heard the smooth rushing sounds of his name, I called to mind not just a warrior chief but the red flowers and green ferns which I'd seen growing all around him, the salt spray of the sea and the silhouette of his steeply sided island. His name was like the sound of clear water running over pebbles, the call of small morning birds. An impossibly blue sky. To me the islands were felt, not said, and although those islands had their voice I would never learn how to speak with it. I could only describe it in my own. Just as I could try to write it down, even though I knew there were no New Zealand words possible in English letters, only the

traces of its sounds left in our language where we'd made
our attempts.

That morning, as we'd watched him paddled away in
chains, was the last time I saw Hara-nui.

Stories came to us afterwards.

We heard that he had been paraded around villages as
an object of derision among the New Zealanders of those
regions. Women gathered together and laughed and threw
things at him as he was forced to walk by. He was taken by
canoe to remote coastal settlements and showed off like
a caught animal before the villagers. Tribes across every
province of Te Rop'raha saw Hara-nui in his shame.

Eventually the Wolf passed him over into the custody
of the wife of Pay-hee, the woman to whom his life was
owed in a price of blood. We heard that for several weeks
Hara-nui lived with her as an honoured guest, that he
was clothed and fed according to his rank. He was not in
irons, nor was he kept tethered or enclosed in a cage. They
lived in this arrangement for some time. And then one day
she ordered her men to take Hara-nui and tie each of his
limbs to the trunks of four separate trees growing close
together, suspending him in midair, stretching him like a
kite. Bound in this way, feeling his arms would be ripped
from out of their sockets, he watched as his captors heated
a long iron rod in the fire. When the metal was hot enough
to set the grass alight they passed it to the wife of Pay-hee.
She approached the prisoner and drove the iron into his
neck. The man screamed and writhed in pain but his bonds
were good and he did not come loose. The men held him

still while the woman placed her mouth over the spring of warm blood and drank from the open wound. Then her son stepped forward and tore the old man's eyes from out of his skull. He swallowed them and with them he consumed all the earthly power of the chief whose soul would never be allowed to rise into the firmament, for he could not see to get there. Never would his eyes be made into stars. When the chief was thoroughly dead his body was cut down and sliced into pieces and eaten.

We heard the story of Hara-nui and Pay-hee's widow from Harvey, a European who lived on the mainland, near Te Rop'raha's northern districts, when we passed through those territories.

We moved north, sharing a cabin in an unfamiliar ship. We had plans to establish a trading station. We would go into the north, he said, to the homeland of the Great Wolf. There is trade waiting to be made there, he said. There were riches of land we could buy, for we'd smuggled things from *Elizabeth* before she sailed, before we'd crept away from her like thieves in the night, stealing back into our dark country where our identities were unknown, erased by the blackness of shadows we journeyed through. We took false names on our passage. He called himself Roberts. It was a blank name, a name that meant nothing to either of us or the lives we'd left behind, or the lives we pictured ourselves moving towards. It was important to take such a name. Though I longed to take a name that meant something to me – Kirkpatrick or Walker, Vittoria or Wolfe – I called myself Radcliff. I named myself after no one I knew. Eventually, in years to come, we would slip back into our true names. But on that trip we were fluid, porous. Our names were gloves we fit inside and then removed, stepped out of. When we changed ships we changed names, we swapped them, becoming each other and becoming one and the same. Even now as I write this I've lost exactly who was who and who was where in this history I have laid down. I existed in the stories he told as he exists only in the words I have written. We were, both of us, the other's device. So in years to come they will say that the one was only the invention of the other. That is how we will seem.

It was years later that another story came to me like a phantom from the *Elizabeth*. She must have been following us for years, that ghost, after she'd been made on the ship we'd left behind. Cowell had never spoken of her, though often my thoughts had gone to her in my quietest most private moments. She was the wife of Hara-nui, the mother of the small girl, young and beautiful, who'd climbed aboard the brig the day the southern chief had been deceived by the white men who'd come to trade with him upon his bay. It had been her mind I'd reached out to over the years, her sadness I'd sought to hold and feel. For she had been forgotten by all those who'd stepped into and out of her story.

And then one day a whisper and an echo of her life was revealed to me. One cold winter afternoon an old whaler passed through our station. We drank with him in the house we'd made for drinking. He recognised Cowell's name. He scoured his memory and told us of that name's part in an infamous past, a native skirmish on an English brig where, it was said, a chief had been clapped in irons and his wife and daughter, also prisoners, brought to him by the war leader Te Rop'raha. The whole family had died horribly, it was said. The chief cut to bits and eaten, the wife the same. But the daughter, she had been strangled by her own parents to save her from a similar fate. Maybe it was just a story, he said. But Cowell said nothing and so that old whaler never knew whether the Cowell he'd met that day and drunk with through that evening was the same Cowell who'd been a youth aboard the bloody *Elizabeth* all those years before.

But for the rest of his life there were nights when Cowell would get drunk and walk again on her deck after dark. Nights when men lay sleeping and he, alert and restless, now an old man with a native wife of his own, passed through the body of his old ship, entering its unlocked cabins, lying in its cots and bunks, trying its cupboards and drawers, talking to himself, talking to me.

Outside in the night the slaughter still happened. It echoed out there even though we'd sailed from it. The still air had carried its clear screams across to us and from down below we'd heard the ship groaning. Wails from deep within her rose as we sailed from Banks.

One night on the return voyage the Watcher and I passed into the fore cabin. He held a lantern before him. In the half-light he checked the cot where the child had lain but there was nothing there, only the empty shape of where her little body had been. When we stood back and turned we saw the wife of Hara-nui holding her daughter, cowered in a corner, and Hara-nui kneeling before them both. The three of them made the shape of a holy sculpture while our quiet flame flickered upon them, their shapes and shadows bound together. The woman slowly lifted her head towards us and we saw that her daughter lay limp in her arms, her skinny limbs dangling like the legs of a slaughtered calf. She held her child out to us and we knew it was dead. The Watcher took the lifeless body from her. When he looked upon the girl he saw that she'd been strangled; he saw the purple black bruises the same size and shape of the impress of a man's thumbs and fingers, a painted necklace around her neck and throat as if she was wearing a choker. The woman spoke to us, at length. Then Hara-nui looked up and said, in English, 'One die; all die.'

We took the body of their dead child away from them. On deck we wrapped her in a sheet and tied the bundle with ropes. We tied heavy stones to her burial shroud. We should have used the native anchor which Evans had stowed below deck but we did not think of it. Clementson removed his hat and we cast her overboard. We did not know her name. We had no prayers.

I cried for the unknown child, and I cried for her mother.

Who was she, that woman whose mind had slid from the map of history and whose words were never understood? How much of her could we explain? What could we tell of her story, her history, from the shape and the colour of the skin of her exposed shoulder in the light of a room where she had held the body of her strangled daughter? Could we dedicate the arc of her hips and breasts, in sorrow, to song? How can we find the perfect words for her and fit them to the shape of her sadness, we, who came with no words she knew or understood? She had been the prow of her people, a gift and an offering. A sacrifice, a struggle, and a game. She had meant all these things but tied none of them together. She was a woman and the wife of a chief who'd come to be all women and all wives to all chiefs, but her expression of whatever longing was purer and more permanent for the way it would slip through its own history, for the way it denied the solid ground, but became rain and fell everywhere.

When she came aboard.
When we went into the hold.
When she strangled her daughter.
When we threw the body into the sea.
Then we had entered each other's histories.

We were received
but now you will devour us.
Your troop has come to tear us apart.

The Wolf is on one island
we are on another.
His island as safe

as if surrounded by swamp.
Made fast by
his men slaughter-cruel.

Now you will devour us; your troop has come to tear
    us apart.

When the Wolf wanders, I suffer.
When the rains came I wept for
when the warrior put his strong arms around me
I loathed myself for the comfort I took.

Wolf. Wolf, I wanted you to come to us.
But in vain I hoped and I, now, am sick with
    mourning
worse than hunger.

This man watching,
does he hear
the heart of my wretched whelp?

Can he hear
the Wolf in the waka
who will carry her to the woods?

My chief and lord would
rather tear us apart.
He would
rather
tear
apart
our song
before it has been sung.

Not easily understood, it was easily done
and our lives
undone.

So her voice comes to us,
a world locked within it
but unlocking another.

Our fate like a gift's, by the giver unvalued:
Friends will assist him if hardship should threaten;
      It is not so with us.

Wulf is on one island, I on another:
His island held safe by a bordering mire;
Warriors dwell there, in battles his comrades—
Friends will assist him if hardship should threaten;
      It is not so with us.
Wulf's days of wandering were my days of torment;
I wept for Wulf when the weather was rainy.
Yet when he clasped me fast in his arms,
My joy was great, but they held grief, too.
Wulf, my Wulf, hoping for you,
For your seldom visit, has brought on me sickness:
The longing of heart, not my hunger for food.

Do you hear, Cradle-Watcher, the lank wolf
Carries our eaglet to the woods.—
Easily a man tears apart what was never joined:
      Our bond is this riddle.

Translated by John F. Adams

Historical Note

While this is a work of fiction, many of the main events described transpired in fact and involved persons whose names have been used in their present recreation. Many sources were useful to me in exploring this fragment of history for my own ends, such as Steven Oliver's entry on Te Rauparaha in *Dictionary of New Zealand Biography* and the Reverend Richard Taylor's account, written in the mid-nineteenth century. With others, these paint a picture of the famed chief as one of the most influential and notable Māori leaders of his day. For a particularly thorough and engaging account of the incident of the brig *Elizabeth* – and one that details the roles of the Captains Stewart and Briggs, the Chief Mate Clementson, and the Trading Master Cowell – Robert McNab's *The Old Whaling Days: A History of Southern New Zealand, from 1830 to 1840*, published in 1913, is available online from the New Zealand Electronic Text Centre.

None of the sources consulted shy away from
the bloodthirsty nature of the times, and though
cannibalism, for instance, has been a contentious issue
in the contemporary representation of the pre-colonial
Māori, I choose to follow the example of the most recent
scholarship which does not dispute its existence but rather
raises questions around the cultural difference which
the practice points to. Further, almost all accounts of
Te Rauparaha and the *Elizabeth* make brief yet peculiar
mention of the haunting fate of the daughter of Te
Maiharanui, as if in her death can be found a talisman of
cultural difference waiting to be understood.

Acknowledgements

Many sources were indispensable to me in the writing
of this novel. Useful biographical information on
Te Rauparaha was found in Steven Oliver's entry, 'Te
Rauparaha ?–1849', in the *Dictionary of New Zealand
Biography*, and Robert Ritchie Alexander's 'Te Rauparaha',
in *Te Ara Encyclopedia of New Zealand*. For a nineteenth-
century English perspective on the exploits of Te
Rauparaha, I leaned heavily on Richard Taylor's *Te Ika
a Maui, or, New Zealand and its inhabitants: illustrating
the origin, manners, customs, mythology, religion, rites,
songs, proverbs, fables, and language of the natives; together
with the geology, natural history, productions, and climate
of the country, its state as regards Christianity, sketches of
the principal chiefs, and their present position*, published in
1855 by Wertheim and Macintosh; the songs on page
42 are based on translations provided by Taylor. I am
indebted also to Robert McNab's books; *Old Whaling Days:*

A History of Southern New Zealand from 1830 to 1840
includes the most thorough account of the incident of
Te Rauparaha and the *Elizabeth* that I could find, including
transcriptions of the sworn depositions of crewmen –
such as John Swan – who bore witness to the historical
massacre, while *Historical Records of New Zealand, Vol.
I* and *Murihiku: A History of the South Island of New
Zealand and the Islands Adjacent and Lying to the South,
from 1642 to 1835* contain evocations and descriptions
of the lives of whalers and traders which I sought to
emulate. McNab's descriptions of Jacky Guard and the
pirate named Walker were particularly instrumental in
my recreation of these historical figures. Other sources
I read and was guided by include Bernard John Foster's
entry, 'Elizabeth, Incident of Brig', in *Te Ara Encyclopedia
of New Zealand*; T. A. Pybus's book *The Maoris of the South
Island*; John White's *The Ancient History of the Maori, his
Mythology and Traditions: Tai-Nui. [Vol. VI]*; and the work
of S. Percy Smith and others, whose book *History and
Traditions of the Taranaki Coast* was originally published
as a series of articles in the *Journal of Polynesian Society*.
Aspects of the lists beginning on page 95 borrow from a
similar and more extensive list that appears in Charles M.
Scammon's *The marine mammals of the north-western coast
of North America, described and illustrated: together with
an account of the American whale-fishery*. The illustration
on page 191 is based on an image of Te Rauparaha's
moko contained in the Blinkensop Deed held at Archives
New Zealand Te Rua Mahara o te Kāwanatanga (NZC
133/5*24/1). Te Rauparaha's haka on pages 78–79 is a

loose interpretation of the famous 'Ka Mate' haka, often attributed to Te Rauparaha, while the lament on page 110 is based on a version of Te Rauparaha's lament for Kawhia, available from *Te Ara Encyclopedia of New Zealand*. I also read many translations of the poem 'Wulf and Eadwacer'. Besides the versions by Richard Hamer and John F. Adams, which appear in this book, I also considered those by Kemp Malone, Janemarie Luecke, Peter Dronke, Jim London, Burton Raffel, and Jack Watson. Bill Manhire's re-invention of the poem, included in his *Collected Poems*, was also drawn upon; Cowell borrows a fragment of the Manhire version on page 87. Many of the above sources offered brief and tantalising glimpses of the historical Cowell, corroborated by scraps of information gathered from the New Zealand Historic Places Trust.

At Penguin, I would like to thank Geoff Walker, Jeremy Sherlock and Frances Faulkner for their professionalism and enthusiasm; also Louise Russell and Jane Parkin who helped edit the revised version of the manuscript. Oliver Stead and Heidi Kuglin offered advice on how to handle potentially sensitive historical subject matter. Mark Williams and Harry Ricketts, my supervisors in another writing life, have been extremely supportive in seeing this book through to publication. Thanks to Jon Duffy, Alan Wightman, Phil O'Brien, Vessy Mark, David Coventry and, most especially, Stephen McDowall, for many enjoyable conversations about the initial idea behind this book and their ongoing encouragement. A special thanks to my friend and collaborator Kirsten Reid, who first suggested to me that someone ought to write a novel based on the poem 'Wulf', and since then has tirelessly read and re-read my numerous drafts and revisions, and helped immeasurably to shape the final book. And finally, thanks to Rosie; this is for you, with love.